RETREAT

Foreword by **KATHLEEN SHOOP**
Edited by **DEMI STEVENS**
Mindful Writers Retreat Authors

"Take a Chance Retreat" – Denise Weaver
"Whispers Beneath the Bridge" – Carol Schoenig
"Lessons from the Girl with the Golden Curls" – Lorraine Donohue Bonzelet
"Chiaroscuro Station" – Deborah Hetrick Catanese
"Saint Ottilia's School for Proper Ladies" – Kimberly Kurth Gray
"Goodnight, Room" – Donna Lucas
"Mystical Mayhem at the Monastery" – Michele Savaunah Zirkle
"On the Corner of Gull Way and Robin Drive" – Amy Morley
"Wine Down Weekend" – Lisa Valli
"Green Thumb" – Melinda Tauler
"A Choice (The Dreamcaster)" – Deborah Hetrick Catanese
"The Bedford Cure" – Kathleen Shoop
"Last Seen in Paradise" – Cindy Hill
"Love's Remains" – Deborah Hetrick Catanese
"Call in Your Ghosts" – Jennifer D. Diamond
"An Apology in Bloom" – Hilary Hauck
"Retreating Within the Silence" – Judy England-McCarthy
"A Certain Magic" – Phil Giunta
"The Perfect Ending" – Gloria Bostic

Print ISBN: 978-1-64649-500-9
Ebook ISBN: 978-1-64649-501-6

Proceeds benefit
House of Ruth Maryland
hruth.org

CONTENTS

FOREWORD

Happy Anniversary to the Mindful Writers Retreat writers and our lucky readers! For 10 years we've gathered in Western Pennsylvania, mostly in Ligonier, to write, meditate, and walk. For writers who are often wedging the crafting of their stories, articles, and books in between family and other work, the ability to retreat from ordinary life provides the chance to start, muddle through middles, and even finish works in progress. Scores of authors have retreated together. Millions of words have been written. Hundreds of books have been born because the Mindful Writers Retreat gives artists the space to create in ways that they can't when subjected to the demands of work and home.

Once the Ligonier-based retreats had taken root, the idea of writing an anthology emerged. Each of the six anthology volumes invites writers to explore different themes or topics. Each anthology calls authors to write in whatever genre they want.

This installment, *Retreat*, is our sixth and it celebrates 10 years and counting. We kept the theme of *Retreat* wide open, so as you read, you'll find that certain stories are clearly about a common understanding of what "retreat" means. Others require you to let the events and characters stew in your mind to get a sense of the author's intentions.

While the Mindful Writers Retreat is only ten years old, the notion of retreating in every form goes back to when humans found a need to rest, restore, and breathe again. Sometimes *retreat* is a formal event. For instance, on military bases "Retreat" is a bugle call that marks the end of the duty day. Military outfits retreat from battles and circumstances to regroup. People retreat from stressful situations or disagreeable "others."

Most religions consider retreating to be an important component of spirituality and retreats are often built into their yearly calendars.

The word "spa" comes from the town of Spa in Belgium where springs were discovered and used for relaxation and curatives since the 1300s. Hot springs, mountaintops, beach towns, and river bends the world over have become spa sites throughout history.

Retreat, however, often means finding a way to insert a little sliver of peace into your schedule. Anyone remember those "Calgon, take me away!" advertisements for bath powder? Sometimes a few minutes of intentional breathing in the woods offers enough decompression on a given day.

We mindful writers consider ourselves very fortunate to have the invitation to carve space into our everyday lives and focus on writing and meditation. Writing alone together, in the company of forests and meals made for us, is a true gift to our writing process.

Readers: we hope you enjoy this anniversary volume that explores a variety of definitions of retreat—nonfiction, fiction, poetry. This collection has it all and we are grateful for your continued support throughout the years. You help make the writing process worth it!

We know how incredibly privileged it is to attend a retreat like ours and that although it is life-changing for people yearning for space to create, there are far more important transformative experiences needed in the world. Many people, especially women and their children, are faced with dire obstacles that make the option to retreat for work or play impossible.

In the notion of retreat and restoration as a lifesaving opportunity, we direct proceeds from *Retreat* to the House of Ruth Maryland. This incredible organization that has been in operation for over four decades "...leads the fight to end violence against women and their children by confronting the attitudes, behaviors, and systems that perpetuate it, and by providing victims with the services necessary to rebuild their lives safely and free of fear" (from hruth.org).

In partnership with Johns Hopkins School of Nursing, they offer an on-site health clinic. They strive to not only provide respite in times of acute need by offering shelter beds, but also have transitional housing and educational programs to give women and families tools to rebuild their lives over time.

So to all the readers who support us, thank you and know that your money is being put to use for something that extends well beyond the moments you enjoy the book.

—Kathleen Shoop

Take a Chance Retreat

Denise Weaver

Doolin House Inn

"**H**ere is the key, Ms. Sullivan. I trust you'll find the room for the Take a Chance Retreat to your satisfaction. Be sure to check out the grand prize basket on your desk."

Maggie Sullivan was still a bit stunned to be on the Emerald Isle, the recipient of a week to write, sightsee, and just soak in the magic of a small country village in Ireland. Ireland! Standing in the place she'd dreamed of going her entire life was almost enough to overcome the pain she felt at the speed that life unfolded, without her consent. She was a manager, a darned good one at that. How could it be that she couldn't manage her own life's plans?

But as always, Maggie switched to the positive tack, choked back grateful tears and focused on the happier things that had transpired in her life. "Thank you, Mr. Higgins. I'm thrilled to be here, of course, but can't believe I won. I'm not truly a writer, you see, so I was shocked to have been awarded this retreat. But believe me, I plan to make good use of my time here."

Higgins nodded, kindness creasing his eyes, and Maggie felt as though perhaps he somehow understood how badly she needed this chance to run away and finally do something she'd long dreamt of doing. Finally, just one thing.

"Your background with bankers, managing teams and corporate events, didn't I just know you would be up to the challenge. But it was the way you described small towns and villages and what they could offer business travelers... I could tell you understood our lives and yearned to experience it yourself. And the writing was grand. Fair play, my dear. You were my choice from the first page I read. Aye, and it's just Higgins, if you please."

Maggie's cheeks went hot. She had never been complimented on her writing before and his reaction reminded her that she really did deserve this trip. She'd nearly missed the deadline to enter the contest from a travel agency she had worked with in organizing corporate travel throughout her career.

For her winning essay, "The Seven Wonders of World Travel," Maggie received a seven-night stay in Doolin, County Clare, Ireland, at the Doolin House Inn, including breakfast and lunch for six days, plus airfare. She was thrilled to win a trip to a place she'd always planned to visit but had not yet fit into her life. Touring Ireland had been part of her long-ago honeymoon plans, but of course, that never transpired. Since airfare was included, and the first week was basically paid, she gifted herself with a second week, hoping to immerse herself in the surroundings as well as writing.

She'd often entertained the idea of writing in retirement, perhaps short stories and essays, a novel, or poetry, possibly a manual for managers. With no ties to home beyond friends and a few former co-workers, Maggie envisioned retirement full of writing and travel.

The pain of losing her parents still caught her off-guard at times. She had overseen their care for the last few years of their lives, starting with her mother's cancer diagnosis and treatments, immediately followed by her dad's quick decline. She'd always been there for them, and never more than in their final years.

While caring for her parents on evenings and weekends, she would take breaks by walking in the woods near their home. A rundown cabin was along her usual path, and she imagined buying and refurbishing it, cooking slow late lunches, photographing deer and birds, recapturing her love for painting. And writing, of course. So many things that could fill her where life had hollowed her out. She'd finally get a dog, one who'd accompany her on walks, lie at her feet, and welcome her home when she returned. Each walk showed her a little more how the life she'd been living all these years hadn't fed her soul.

Winning the retreat came at just the right time. She'd taken early retirement, but was a little unmoored by having no schedule, no real responsibilities, not yet taking action to make any of her dreams come to life. She hadn't even inquired about buying the cabin in the woods. Secure with a good retirement package and a modest inheritance from her parents, she was left floundering when she should have been relieved. This trip was her opportunity to immerse herself and see if she could make writing work.

Her real dream was to pen a mystery novel set in both Ireland and Italy, one that had a little romance, as well as food and music as side characters. While she hadn't had much time for travel herself, she'd voyaged a million miles while planning trips for senior level managers. The work gave her an understanding of the finer points of travel.

Now here she was, in lovely Doolin, Ireland, along the Wild Atlantic Way in County Clare. In addition to the breathtaking scenery, delicious food, and celebratory people, Maggie had learned that Doolin was known as the home of traditional Irish music. She was looking forward to participating in it all—nature, warmth and hospitality from local folks, amazing food, along with music and stories every night in the pub—definitely great *craic*. A bank manager who regaled her with stories from his business trip to Dublin shared with Maggie the term *craic* meant fun or a good time. She thought it would be wonderful to have the opportunity to experience this firsthand.

Maggie settled into the retreat. It was organized as a self-guided time away for writing, renewal, and inspiration. Previously, she had arranged for two members of the bank's foundation to attend a Mindful Writers Retreat in a lovely rural, wooded setting not far from Pittsburgh. She had learned that at those retreats, one of the mainstays was mindful walking each day wherein the writer allowed nature and the rhythm of the walk to flow through her body and mind, providing fertile space for creativity to flourish. Maggie tucked that concept away in her memory, hoping to someday find herself in a similar retreat. So now, she brought this aspect of the Pennsylvania retreats with her to Ireland and was using it faithfully each day.

On her first early morning walk just before daybreak, Maggie noticed an inviting Bed & Breakfast called Cottage O'Connell. She inched closer, then stopped, awed. It had a lovely gray stone façade with an inviting red door for the main entrance and red window frames, surrounded by wildflowers. It was as though her cabin in the woods had materialized in Ireland, fully renovated in the fashion she would do back home. Then a light went on in the kitchen so she dashed away, worried she'd be arrested for peeping in the windows. The next morning, she intentionally walked past it again, feeling an unusual rush of contentedness, stopping again to take in the beauty, to inspire her dreams.

Later that afternoon, needing a break from the story she was working on, Maggie went walking. As she approached the cottage, she saw a lovely woman with ginger, windblown hair, strands torn from the ribbon at the nape of her neck. She was cutting flowers from the garden. Her sky-blue dress flowed about her, tamped down in the front by a worn apron with pockets, and a basket was hooked over her arm with yellow roses and white lilies cascading over the edges. Maggie heard the trickle of a stream meandering over stones coming from nearby, and wished she could sit on the grayed wooden bench next to the fragrant roses and take in all the beauty.

Maggie started to walk on, then paced back. "Excuse me... I know this is weird, but I just wanted to say how much I love the appearance of your place. It's so quaint and, well, just lovely," Maggie said. "Magic."

The owner walked the few steps to the gate and extended her hand. "I'm Cara. Are you the one who's been past in the mornings?"

Maggie gasped, "I'm so sorry but—"

Cara chuckled and shook her head. "It's so nice to meet you. Thank you for the compliment. I'm trying hard to keep up with things here. It's me home and business."

"I must tell you, it just captivates me. Inexplicably. If I were to conjure up a home, this would be it." Feeling awkward for being so forward, Maggie thought she should explain herself. "I'm a guest at the Doolin House Inn, staying the rest of this week and all of next."

Cara nodded and smiled. "That's grand. Would you like to call round tomorrow afternoon for a cup of tea and some muffins? I can give you a little tour. I've some guests to welcome shortly, but tomorrow afternoon I'll be free."

Maggie eagerly accepted and they agreed on a time. Her steps back to the inn were light and bouncy, dizzy with the idea of seeing the cottage. Perhaps she could bring these elements to the cabin in the woods back home?

"Higgins, what can you tell me about Cottage O'Connell?" Maggie asked when she returned to the inn just in time for breakfast.

"Ah, a sad tale there, my dear. Let me get the rest of the guests seated and I'll join you for coffee, if you'd like. I can tell you all about it." Thirty minutes later, as Maggie relished the last bite of her scone with clotted cream and berry jam, Mr. Higgins joined her. She poured them each a cup of coffee from the tableside carafe.

"Well, I promised you a tale, didn't I? I'll start at the beginning, which is always the best place, don't you think?"

Maggie agreed and got more settled in her seat.

"The cottage belonged to several generations of the McCauley family. As times changed and families grew, the McCauleys moved on to Dublin and the cottage became a seldom-used family retreat."

"Then Cara, the only granddaughter of the last McCauley to live here, married a smart young man, Rory

O'Connell. They refurbished the cottage and opened it as a Bed & Breakfast. Rory and Cara lived there, planning to build a separate home as they had children. Sadly, no children arrived and eventually they gave up on the dream of a large family and remained in the cottage."

Maggie nodded ever so slightly, with her brow creased. "That is sad." She pressed her hand to her chest. Life had swept by quickly and along with it took any promise of having her own family.

Higgins continued, "That's not the saddest part. Late last year Rory passed away. The dreaded cancer. So now Cara is alone, trying to keep up the B&B and get through each day. She's such a sweet thing, only early forties and alone. No husband. No children. A truly sad story."

Maggie exhaled. She was her own sad story. And she suddenly knew how people must have viewed her. She'd basically turned into a spinster, all work and almost no play, and then adding on the responsibility of caretaker for her mother and father.

Maggie's gaze slipped to every corner and plane of Cara's home. Flowers in vases and potted ivy, antique platters on the walls and stoneware bowls full of glass balls and granite paperweights. A home curated with love and filled with things that may have been clutter to someone else but were pure magic in this house. The afternoon flew by as Maggie and Cara had an instant connection and chatted away like long-lost friends renewing a sisterly friendship. Over famous Barry's Irish tea and moist, tender raspberry muffins, they talked of careers and family, love and loss.

Maggie couldn't believe what she was revealing about her life as a single but once-engaged woman. Her fiancé died tragically in a car accident several months before their wedding nearly twenty years before. Despite the tragedy and never finding love again, she was grateful she'd been able to care for her parents when they needed her, and took pride in her successful career.

Cara's husband had been a trained chef but didn't like restaurant life. He and Cara purchased her family cottage and opened the B&B. Rory had a real business sense and they always had a full house of paying guests thanks to his adept website and social media skills.

"Rory was so good with the guests, too. He prepared delicious breakfasts each day, including the full Irish, of course, and offered lunch specials by request, things like picnic basket lunches and boxed sandwiches to go. Also soups and salads to eat here. He kept up with all the internet things and the reservations, taxes, all that business stuff that I fear is over my head."

Cara was good with gardening and cleaning, tasks she could lose time and thought while doing, and it suited her well. She was happy with those chores. But cooking was just not in her wheelhouse, and she was out of her depths when it came to the business end of things, especially technology. She just wasn't sure she could handle it all. In fact, she knew she couldn't.

"Maggie, I can't believe I'm spilling my insides to you like this. We've only just met... you must think me rather dotty."

"Oh, Cara, not at all. You've been through so much, caring for your husband during his illness and then his passing. Obviously, you can't, and shouldn't, continue doing the work of two people. Can you hire some help?"

"I know that's what I need, but I'm so bad at the numbers—I'm not sure I can afford it. I'm in bits about it most of the time." She and Rory had always been happy with their modest income, not having children to support and no wishes for extravagance. "We never lived the grand life; we didn't need much. But I don't even know if I'm losing money now."

Cara shook her head, stamped a foot and said, "Enough of that. I'm sorry. You're here on a holiday of sorts and you don't need to hear my sob story. I'll be fine, I have to be. I'll do it for Rory."

Maggie hugged Cara tight. "I'm pulling for you, and I have faith in you."

As she returned to the inn for dinner and an evening of writing, Maggie glimpsed a dog peering around the corner of the B&B. She glanced back, but either it was gone, or she'd imagined it.

That evening Maggie could not concentrate on her writing, and she slept fitfully during the night. The next morning, she arose before dawn, dressed, and went out to walk. She'd intended to avoid Cottage O'Connell, just trying to get her mind back on her writing.

"Focus, focus," she said to herself. "*Murder and Mayhem in an Irish Monastery.* Too much alliteration? Title comes last. You need to write the story."

She trailed through the village, thinking of plot lines and characters. Realizing her shoe had come untied, Maggie bent to retie it. As she was standing again, she thought she heard a dog bark. Looking around, she was astounded to see she was once more near Cottage

O'Connell, and wasn't that a red-haired dog behind one of the rose bushes?

She started toward the cottage, calling softly, "Here puppy, come here sweet boy." The dog eyed her warily. Just as Maggie put her hand on the gate, the dog produced a deep-throated bark and placed itself between the gate and the cottage front door.

"It's okay, boy. I just want to say hello."

From the cottage, Cara's voice called out, "Oliver, it's okay, I'm coming." Stepping out onto the sidewalk, Cara saw Maggie and apologized. "I'm sorry, I hope he didn't frighten you."

"No, I'm fine. But he obviously was not going to allow me to trespass. Not that that was what I was doing! I just saw him and wanted to pet him. I love dogs. What happened to his leg?"

"We don't know. I don't know. Oliver appeared one evening, not long after Rory's diagnosis. Poor fella was missing his front leg, but the area had already healed. No one knew who he belonged to or how he may have gotten here. He kept coming back. So of course, we started feeding him, and in short order, he became our dog and Rory's near constant companion."

"Did your husband name him?" Maggie asked softly.

"Yes, *Oliver Twist* was one of his favorite books and thought perhaps somehow the dog had lived a similar life and was now hoping to live happily and safely in the country. Oliver seemed to like the name and that was that. Now since Rory is gone, Oliver feels like my protector. I swear Rory made the dog promise to watch over me."

Maggie thought of how she'd wanted a pet to care for, and how she would spend days in the woods. Making a garden at the cabin perhaps? Though Cara had lost her husband, she'd created a sanctuary that inspired Maggie. "Well, I'm glad you have a protector, and he's a handsome one at that. Irish Terrier, right?"

"Yes, you know your dogs."

"Well, I'm no expert, but back home in the States I do enjoy watching the various dog competitions and recognize many breeds."

Cara opened the gate, soothing Oliver, and invited Maggie to come into the garden. "Would you like to pet him?"

Maggie practically jumped at the chance, and as she knelt, Oliver planted a slobbery kiss on her cheek, nearly knocking her over.

"I think he approves," Cara said, chuckling.

"I think I do too."

Two days later, after two more nights of fitful sleep, Maggie had come to a decision. After breakfast, she marched over to Cottage O'Connell, and after Oliver's announcement that she was approaching, she opened the gate and knocked on the door.

Cara opened it looking frazzled, flour dusted over her apron, her lovely red hair falling out of the braid she typically wore, and what looked like blueberry smudges on her hand and cheek.

"Oh, Maggie, so nice to see you. But I'm sorry I don't have time to talk just now."

"Cara, that's fine, because I want to do the talking anyway. Can you join me tonight for dinner at Gus O'Conner's pub? My treat. I've been here almost a week and still haven't gone. I know it's the oldest pub in the area and I've heard the food is divine. Will you?"

"I must say, that would be lovely. Okay, yes, I will." Cara sighed, brushed the flour from her apron and repeated with determination, "Yes, I will!"

They talked over a superb dinner of stuffed mushrooms as an appetizer followed by O'Conner's fresh battered fish and chips with mushy peas. Despite the name, she thought even the mushy peas were delicious. They ended the meal with warm apple crumble and an Irish coffee.

As they ate, the two new friends talked of hobbies and food, childhood and family. The meal was wonderful, the live music entertaining, and the ambiance warm and friendly. Maggie learned that the name Cara was Irish for *friend*. How appropriate.

"And your name, Maggie... you do know how very popular that is here in Ireland, don't you?"

"I thought it might be. I'm named for a great-aunt, Margaret Kelly. She was my mother's favorite aunt and lived here in Ireland. I never had the chance to meet her, but my mother spoke often of her dear Aunt Maggie."

They finished about 9:15 and Maggie asked if they could walk to the Doolin Pier to see the Cliffs of Moher, only a nineteen-minute stroll. She'd heard that it was a great experience to see the cliffs at night, this time of year when the sun didn't set until nearly 10:00 PM.

As they made their way to the pier, Maggie hesitantly brought up the conversation she was both eager and reluctant to have.

"Cara, I don't want to impose, especially since we really only met, but I think I can help with your B&B, if you'd like, I mean."

Cara looked away.

Maggie grabbed her hand. "Hear me out, please. I have another week here, and only if you want, I could take a look at your books for you, your online presence and reservation system. It's what I did for twenty years. I can assess where things stand for you."

Cara met her gaze, but Maggie couldn't read her thoughts. "Before you say no, please be assured you can trust me. I have references. You can check me out. No charge to you. You need a break, and I need to do something that will make me feel good, that will fill my soul a bit."

Midway through Maggie's offer, Cara's mouth went agape. "Are you serious like?"

"I don't know what it is, but you feel like family, and..." *I need family* is what she wanted to say, but didn't. "I want to help. But I go home at the end of next week."

"Am I hearing this correctly? You want to help? For no reason?"

"For you."

"This is too generous!" Cara choked out. "You're here to write, to be inspired. I can't ask you to give up that time and opportunity. This was a dream for you, and you must take advantage of it. I'll be okay. I'll figure it out."

Maggie wagged her head. "No. This is something I want to do much more. I don't know, but I feel compelled to help and I have no doubt that this is the right thing. The right thing for you. The right thing for me. If you trust me."

Cara scratched Oliver under his chin. "Oliver's acceptance of you is enough," she sighed. "Yes, if you are absolutely sure this is what you want to do." She wiped away tears. "Thank you so much. I don't think I'll ever be able to really say thank you."

Over the next four days, Maggie pored over the books, the B&B's website and social media pages, and the reservation system. She found a few glitches that were easily fixed by software updates. The financials looked to be in fairly good order, though a bit behind in reconciliations.

"Good news, Cara. You are in better shape than you thought. You actually can afford to get some part-time help. My recommendation would be to hire someone to do the cooking. Maybe cut back a little on the special lunches at first to see how things go.

"And, if you want, I can occasionally update your social media pages for you from my home in Pennsylvania until you feel more comfortable doing it yourself. Or you could talk to the local college and see about setting up an internship with a student. There are possibilities."

"Oh, Maggie, you are an amazing friend. Thank you, thank you, thank you!"

"I can't tell you how happy it has made me to do this work. I still have time for writing before I need to leave. I have the rest of my life. To be honest, though, I'm not excited about leaving. I love it here."

"Ireland has a way of doing that to people." Cara grinned.

"There's good reason." Closing her eyes, Maggie spun around like a child. "This place is magical."

Maggie spent her remaining time journaling, outlining, writing, and hiking. It had been different than she expected, but glorious. As she packed she finally took time to go through all the little treasures left for her in the prize basket that had been provided by the contest sponsor. Among the chocolates, bath salts, and scarves, she found an All Cash Spectacular Irish lottery ticket. Well, that was interesting.

She pocketed the ticket and headed to Cara's.

Over a bowl of lamb stew and brown bread, Maggie and Cara expressed their appreciation for the newfound friendship.

Maggie cleared her throat. "I have a little something for you." She reached into her pocket to retrieve the scratch-off ticket, but it was gone. Disappointed, she explained to Cara about the gift basket and the lottery ticket. "I wanted to give you the ticket. I have no idea if it would have been lucky or not," she said with a shrug.

"I couldn't have taken it, Maggie. You've already done so much."

"Moot point now that I've lost it. And I couldn't have collected had it been a winner. You have to be a legal resident of Ireland to receive any lottery winnings. Oh well, it was fun to think about."

As they were clearing the table and saying their goodbyes, Oliver created a ruckus outside, barking and jumping, scratching at the door. Cara opened the door and Oliver trotted in on his three legs, tail wagging, head held high with something in his mouth.

Cara squealed as she took the object from Oliver. "It's your lottery ticket, Maggie! It must have fallen out of your pocket as you walked here and Oliver found it. Good boy, Oliver, good boy!"

"I'll say," Maggie agreed. "Sadly, I really have to run to gather my things and catch my ride to the airport. Tonight, when you're relaxed, have an Irish coffee and scratch that ticket. I wish you all good luck. Maybe you'll be a winner."

"Maggie, I already feel like I am a winner. I had a loving marriage, I have a nice business here, I have Oliver, and now I have a friend in America."

"And I have a wonderful friend in Ireland." Maggie sniffed, dabbed at a few tears, and slowed her breathing, trying to quell the fluttering in her chest. "I feel revived. There are still things I can do, and who knows what adventures lay before me. Thank you, Cara, for helping me see this."

A few days later, Maggie was getting settled back in at home in Pittsburgh, scrolling through the real estate info for that old cabin, wondering if it would work as she envisioned. Her phone buzzed. A text from Cara. "CALL ME!" No explanation, just the request for a call.

"Cara, so nice to hear from you. I hope all is well."

"You won't believe it. I talked to a solicitor today. It will work. I'm so excited, I can't believe it."

"Cara, slow down. What will work?"

"I have a proposition. Are you sitting down? Please sit down. This is big news. You know that lottery ticket? It was a winner. Not only a winner, but it was the top prize of 200,000 euros. 200,000!"

"Oh, Cara, I'm so thrilled for you. I truly could not be happier. I only wish I were there to hug you and to celebrate with you!"

"But Maggie, wait. My proposition. I cleared it all with the solicitor. Maggie…"

"What? What? Spill it!"

"Will you be my business partner?

"Your... business?"

"Don't say no. Just like when you told me not to say no to you. Do you trust me? I have references."

Maggie's eyes filled. She couldn't get the words out.

"Move here, be my business partner, and write your novel and all the other projects you want to do. Will you do it?"

Maggie, breathing deeply but not hesitating, replied, "Yes, Cara. I will."

WHISPERS BENEATH THE BRIDGE

Carol Schoenig

"There will be no more extensions. If you can't produce the novel, we'll cancel the contract and you'll need to repay the advance," said editor Julie Swatch.

Claire Houston had been grappling with the fear of losing her sense of identity as an artist. After years of pouring herself into her work, she found herself paralyzed by the thought her creative well had run dry, leaving her with nothing left to give. "I don't know what to do. How can I restore my creative spark?"

"Hmm."

She heard typing.

"Ah, here it is. There is this unique retreat place, dedicated to creative types. It's in New Wilmington, Pennsylvania. A small Amish town. I'm suggesting you go there. It has a story of its own. At least that's what the advertisement says." Julie paused. "I'll send this over to you."

The next day, Claire stood on the wooden planks of the Airbnb that creaked beneath her boots. The smell of cedar and aged wood wrapped around her like a fragile blanket. She paused, taking a deep breath that felt heavier than it should have. This place, a covered bridge over a quiet creek, had become a rustic home.

She tried to escape the suffocating grip of creative paralysis. Deadlines loomed like storm clouds, dark and unrelenting, as the blinking cursor on her laptop mocked her empty thoughts. Her ability to conjure worlds with ease, and weave characters and emotions into stories that felt alive, was unlimited. But now? Every idea felt lifeless. She forced every word.

Her editor's reminders had turned from gentle nudges to pointed warnings. The pressure to deliver the novel she'd promised—a sweeping tale of love, betrayal, and redemption—gnawed at her daily.

A breakup with the man she thought she'd spend her life with had left her heart brittle and her confidence shattered. Writing, once her solace, now felt like a punishment. Each sentence echoed her ex's voice, teasing her to escape reality into fantasy worlds.

Perhaps here, away from the chaos of her life, she could discover the peace she sought. Maybe she could reclaim her muse and meet the deadline before everything fell apart.

The quiet was mesmerizing and disturbing in its intensity, pressing against her like a held breath. Excitement surged.

She unpacked her writing bag, arranging her tablets and pens on the worn wooden table. No Wi-Fi. No distractions. That was the point. Just her, the words she hoped to find, and the blank page daring her to fill it. But the sight of the empty tablet made her stomach knot.

As Claire wandered the room, her fingers traced the rough-hewn beams and the edges of a braided rug that softened the wooden floor. The walls displayed vibrant paintings; their brushstrokes were bold yet tender, a storm of color against the muted simplicity of the space. The owner's artistry, she mused, sparked her longing for such assured creativity. A picture of a tall, handsome man standing in front of the bridge caught her attention. The smile on his face was teasing and playful. He must have posed for the artist.

Outside, the hum of crickets rose in harmony with distant owl calls, the smell of honeysuckle mingling with damp earth. Tranquility drew Claire to the small porch where she stepped out. The creek below shimmered in the moonlight, its gentle babble a balm for her jangled nerves. She leaned against the railing, letting herself breathe, until a movement in the water caught her eye.

She gasped, and a shiver of panic went up her spine. A face—sharp, semi-familiar—reflected in the rippling surface.

Claire froze, her breath caught in her throat. When she looked again, the object had disappeared, leaving the water undisturbed. She pressed her hands against the railing, forcing herself to breathe. Exhaustion, she thought, though her pounding heart betrayed her rationalization.

She returned to the kitchen and occupied herself with the simple task of preparing a sandwich and tea. Each motion was a minor rebellion against the unease creeping in. Yet her eyes kept drifting to the writing tools on the table. She wanted the distraction, the escape, but shaking her head, she reminded herself why she was there. She opened the device and stared at the screen. The emptiness taunted her; the words refused to come.

Frustrated, she slumped over the table, her head resting against the cool wood. In the stillness, her mind wandered, unbidden images of the bridge in its prime filling the void. She imagined walking its length, a ghostly wind tugging at her coat until a loud gust rattled the shutters and blew the door open.

An unusual illumination outlined a man standing in the doorway. As Claire forced herself to stand, her heart raced and her breath caught. "Who are you?" she asked, her voice hushed.

The man stepped forward, his presence solid yet ethereal. "My name is Nathaniel." His voice was deep, but gentle.

"You're the man in the painting."

"Yes. Eleanor painted that picture. This is what I wish to discuss."

Claire put her hand up to her heart. "I must be hallucinating that a ghost is talking to me."

"I have a story to tell you."

Claire swallowed hard, curiosity mingling with apprehension. "What kind of tale?"

"A declaration of love." His sorrowful gaze met hers. "A tragic one."

Her body tensed as the chill from outside seeped into the room. Nathaniel picked up the throw from over the rocker and draped it around her shoulders. His touch was firm yet like the brush of a feather. He gestured to the porch, and despite the hammering in her chest, Claire followed.

The air was dense as they sat quietly, she in the chair and he on the steps. She broke the silence. "Why has this happened to me?"

His gaze lingered on the creek, the moonlight casting shadows across his face. "Aren't you here to write?"

She nodded, wary yet intrigued. "How do you know that?"

"I've seen many travelers come and go," he said. "Few stay long enough to listen. Yet, I detected your intrigue and sensed... you might empathize."

His voice softened as he began his tale, weaving together fragments of love and loss. The story of Eleanor unfolded, her spirit lingering on the bridge, her vibrant paintings hidden within its boarded walls. As Nathaniel spoke, the weight of his grief pulled Claire in like the current of the creek below.

He sighed, looking toward the moonlit creek. "I was a carpenter. I helped build the bridge in the early 1900s. This bridge... it's where I met the love of my life."

His voice softened further still. "It was a stormy evening when Eleanor found refuge beneath the bridge. The storm soaked her to the bone. Her pale pink dress clinging to her figure, her golden hair plastered to her face. A heavenly being. She was incongruous with her surroundings. She spoke with warmth, inquisitiveness—something that ignited my heart."

Claire watched him, absorbed in his memories. Pain etched deep into his features, but there was a gentleness in his tone that drew her in.

"She was the cherished daughter of the Harrington family, owners of grand estates and vast lands. Spirited and kind, but trapped by her family's expectations. That night, as the storm raged, we shared stories and laughter. For a few hours, we weren't a carpenter and heiress. We were just... us."

He hesitated, his hands gripping the arms of the rocker. "We met again, and again. She found excuses to wander near the bridge, and I... I dreamed of those moments. Each meeting served as a defiance of the world we entered. I'd bring her small gifts—wildflowers, carved trinkets. I built walls, a roof, and windows over the bridge so that she could paint during inclement weather. She taught me of far-off places, ideas that felt impossible."

Nathaniel's voice had grown heavier as his tale darkened. "But word spread. Her father found out. Charles Harrington saw me as nothing more than a penniless dreamer. He arranged her engagement to Edward Gainsborough, an heir with wealth and influence."

Nathaniel's voice cracked. "We tried to fight it. Letters passed through a kind housemaid. Clandestine plans in the shadows. But Charles intercepted one of my letters. He sent men to the bridge to warn me. That night, I waited for Eleanor. She never came."

The burden of his words hung in the air. Claire shivered again, her throat tight. "What happened to her?"

"Her father insisted she marry Edward Gainsborough, a man as cold as the estate they would share. But Eleanor's heart defied those commands."

"Weeks passed, and I received a note from her. I imagined her writing it. She pleaded that she couldn't bear the idea of marrying Edward."

Nathaniel's voice faltered. "I couldn't stand the thought of her harming herself. I crafted a plan that would let us run away together to start anew."

He breathed deeply, his gaze distant. "On the eve of her wedding, she met me under the bridge. We were starting our plan when a flash flood struck. The current was overwhelming. I struggled to hold on to her, but the swift water proved too much. We made it to the edge, clinging to a branch, my arm around her waist, as we braved the storm together. We spoke of love, of the life we dreamed of—until the water pulled us away."

His eyes filled with unshed tears, his voice choked. "In the morning, they found us. Our arms wrapped around each other as we drowned."

"The order came to separate us. Even if it meant cutting my body away from her. Our spirits saw and heard everything that was happening. Knowing that we could reconnect no matter what, we agreed to separate rather than have our bodies destroyed. We let go.

"Regret and guilt consumed Charles Harrington, leaving him in a state of such utter despair that he had the bridge boarded up and closed. Later, he provided the funds to build another bridge further down the river. Even after our spirits separated, we remained tethered to this place. Our home."

"But why stay here?"

"The land itself holds unresolved echoes of our history. It holds our memories, the unspoken regrets and moments of joy. This is where our love story began. Our essence lingers in the spaces we loved, waiting for someone to understand and honor our story."

"But how did it come to be an Airbnb?" Claire asked.

"After losing Eleanor, her father became distraught, losing some of his mental abilities. Over time, their finances deteriorated. He couldn't bear the thought of leaving the estate, especially the boarded-up bridge."

Pausing, he added, "Its beauty and peace drew artists, writers, and other creatives to the town." Nathaniel turned to Claire, his face lined with grief. "I'm running out of time. Eleanor's paintings... they deserve to be seen." He looked into Claire's eyes. "She even painted some after death."

Claire recalled reading about paintings that appeared by magic on forgotten canvases or walls in the estate's studio—out of nowhere. She remembered the electric atmosphere of the makeshift house.

The smell of jasmine—Eleanor's favorite flower—drifted through the air, followed by the faint strains of a melody only she had played on the piano before her death.

The newer paintings, however, had taken a surreal turn. They depicted imagery that couldn't have existed during her life—modern visitors to the estate, landmarks that emerged long after her death, or stormy skies swirling with ghostly figures.

An intimate gallery room within the house displayed these works, light filtering through cracked, colored-glass windows, casting an unworldly glow over the collection. Visitors claimed that standing before these paintings evoked a deep connection, as though Eleanor herself spoke to them, urging them to uncover the hidden meanings in her brushstrokes.

"I want her work viewed and purchased. Repairing our home, the covered bridge, requires money. Can you help us?"

The night deepened, and Claire's doubts about her purpose and her words faded. Eleanor's unrelenting passion for painting—even beyond death—both inspired and haunted her. The message in Eleanor's brushstrokes felt clear: You cannot stop creating.

At 3:30 AM, overcome by exhaustion, Claire rested her head on the table. When she awoke three hours later, she found her papers spread out in front of her. Odd—she had stacked them in a neat pile the night before. She glanced around the room, searching for the source of the honey-like scent.

She rose from the chair, stretched, and began putting the pages back in order. Gathering them, she gasped—

someone had circled words in red and scribbled notes in the margins. Goosebumps appeared on her arms. Someone had read her work. But who? The scent of jasmine still hung in the air, a ghostly mist of Eleanor's presence.

She ate breakfast before taking coffee onto the veranda. Below, the river swirled, mesmerizing her. She lingered by the railing, scanning the misty water for any sign of Nathaniel. But the river held only its silent secrets. With a sigh, she turned and stepped back inside, hoping that immersing herself in her writing might ease the heaviness in her chest.

She had written a haunting tale of forbidden love and its power to endure against all obstacles.

Inside the house, she made one last check to ensure she had left nothing behind. As she turned to leave, her steps faltered.

An unseen painting leaned in the room's far corner.

Her breath caught.

She stood beside a slim, light-haired man. He was a stranger to her. Their intimate, knowing stare held each other.

A folded note lay there, waiting for her.

Heart pounding, Claire reached for it.

Thank you for helping us. Our spirits have reunited.

Your perfect match exists. When you least expect it, he will appear.

Claire ran her fingers over the words. A prickling sensation coursed through her.

She turned, half-expecting to see Nathaniel standing there, watching her with that gentle, knowing smile. But the room remained silent. The air was still.

A tranquil peace settled over her. She felt grounded, a first in months. Nathaniel and Eleanor had found their closure. And so had she.

She'd come here feeling lost, not knowing who she was without her stories or love. But now, something had shifted. The words were within reach. Her heart no longer felt empty.

Claire stood at the edge of the bridge, the old wood creaking beneath her boots. The lantern in her hand flickered, casting long shadows across the misty water below. Behind her, the cabin's windows glimmered, but she knew this would be her last night here.

Nathaniel stood beside her, more translucent than he had been before. His features, once sharp and defined, were now blurred at the edges, as though time were finally loosening its grip on him.

"You're leaving," he said.

Claire nodded, her throat tight. "It's time."

She had finished the manuscript—the story of Nathaniel and Eleanor, a truth long buried. The missing pieces had come together: Eleanor's final painting, the letters hidden within the cabin, the whispers that had guided her. The prospect of leaving this place pained her.

Nathaniel smiled. "You have done more for me than you realize."

"But what happens to you now?" she whispered.

The wind picked up, rustling the trees. Nathaniel turned his gaze toward the water below, his expression unreadable. "I don't know," he admitted. "But I feel... lighter." He exhaled, and his breath came as a mist drifting away into the cold air. "Perhaps telling our story was enough."

Claire reached for him on impulse, her fingers passing through his own. Briefly, she felt something. A whisper of warmth, the faintest brush of contact.

"I'll never forget you," she said. There was something in his eyes—gratitude. Or peace.

Nathaniel inclined his head. "Nor I you."

A final gust of wind swept across the bridge, carrying the last echoes of his presence with it. Claire blinked, and when she looked again, Nathaniel was gone. The bridge stood silent beneath her feet, the night still and waiting.

She took a deep breath and clutched her manuscript to her chest. It was time to leave.

The bookstore was warm and bustling, the scent of paper and coffee mingling in the air. Claire adjusted the stack of books on the table, smoothing her hands over the embossed title: *Whispers Under the Bridge.*

"You're the author," a voice declared from across the table.

The man standing there evoked a strong sense of recognition. He stood tall, boasting light-colored hair and piercing blue eyes. He looked oddly familiar.

He glanced at the book in her hands, then back at her with a crooked smile.

"I'm familiar with the setting in your book."

Claire's heart pounded. "You?" She shook her head. Her heart raced, wondering if this was a joke. Was he the spirit who addressed her?

"I'm James Hovert," the man introduced himself, extending his hand. "I've read your book. Fascinating story. Actually..." After a moment of hesitation, he took something out of his pocket—a folded piece of paper that carried a hint of jasmine. "I discovered this in an old bookstore."

Claire unfolded the page with trembling fingers. The drawing depicted Eleanor and Nathaniel... Claire's gaze lifted.

James watched her, a trace of wonder in his eyes.

"You look like him," she whispered.

He tilted his head, unsure. "So I've been told. Nathaniel was... a distant relative, apparently. But I never knew much. My family never talked about him."

The air between them shimmered with something unspoken. As if threads long severed had woven themselves back together in this quiet moment.

"May I buy you a cup of coffee?" he asked.

Claire exhaled, the weight of the past easing—just a little. Was this a coincidence? Destiny? Or Nathaniel's last gift?

She smiled. "I'd love that."

LESSONS FROM THE GIRL
WITH THE GOLDEN CURLS

Lorraine Donohue Bonzelet

Daria cringed listening to the screeching grind that the metal base of the table made as she dragged it across the floor. She positioned the piece of furniture in front of the bay window, equidistant between her two loves: the old soot-stained stone fireplace and the sugar-stacked snack table.

She removed the shrink wrap from the rainbow-colored index cards and placed them next to the mounded assortment of pens. Urged by sheepish curiosity, Daria glanced around to see how the other writers were setting up their workspaces. The large rec room was bustling with vitality. *A full week of writing. No distractions. No cleaning. No cooking. No dishes.* A rush of goosebumps dotted her arms. Daria dumped the remaining contents of her backpack onto the table: writing shawl, sea-turtle mug, a bergamot candle, and, for giggles, the eight-inch statue of a meditating giraffe that her sister had gifted her. She smirked with satisfaction.

Daria ran her fingers through her tangled web of frizzy curls. The only task remaining was to awaken her creative muse. She wasn't sure she would know a muse if she came smack dab face-to-face with it, but she needed to try.

Settling into her chair, she admired the crimson and ginger streams of sunrise behind the mountainous landscape. Daria massaged a labradorite crystal in her left hand and sodalite in her right. She closed her eyes and mentally enclosed herself in a deep blue aura. Her hands swirled the crystals in front of her throat, imitating a podcast she'd recently watched. Daria reminded herself, *This motion energizes the chakra of communication and creativity.* With a gentle outward twist of her wrist, she opened her palms, presenting the crystals upward to the sky. She released their energy out to the universe.

Daria heard a light tap at the window. Then another tap, slightly louder. Determined to ignore the rude and untimely interruption, she squeezed her eyes tighter.

The taps grew more frequent and louder still. Daria peeked one eye open to spot a little girl's golden-bronze curls bobbing up and down. The girl turned toward the window, showcasing an adorable dimpled smile. With a mischievous but welcoming glint in her eyes, she signaled for Daria to follow. She skipped down the path toward the red oaks and eastern hemlocks at the far side of the grassy knoll. The girl with the golden curls paused often to look back at Daria.

Her skip was exaggerated, lifting her little body several inches off the ground. Lanky arms and legs flopped loose and carefree. She looked like a rag doll tossing about. When she landed, her bare feet squished into the mud left over from the previous night's thunderstorm. *The joy of running barefoot is a natural instinct for children*, Daria thought. *For adults, it is an odd and purposeful action called barefooting.* Daria was tempted to remove her shoes too, for she'd read about the benefits of walking barefoot, but the thought of goopy mud seeping between her toes... *Eww! No thanks!*

Daria stood at the forest's edge, under a tall dew-dripping conifer tree. She was stricken with caution and panic. *Why is this child running amok, barefoot, barely sunrise, in this remote and densely wooded forest— without an adult in sight?*

The little girl, no more than five, popped out from behind the cinnamon-brown bark of a hemlock. She wiggled her finger signaling for Daria to follow. Then she sprinted away.

Who is she and why is she luring me into the forest? Dummy, the real question is: why are you naively following?

"Wait up!" Daria yelled, ignoring those nagging thoughts.

Not twenty feet into the shadowy woodlands, with towering red oaks surrounding her, Daria had second thoughts. She turned to go back to the retreat center. She thought it was a wiser decision to let the retreat staff find the missing girl... until... thick vines of verdant ivy fell from the trees. They intertwined and braided, weaving upward and outward, creating an impenetrable wall that closed off the path. Daria skittered left and right looking for an opening. Thin ivy tendrils slithered forward, wrapping around her ankles. Daria broke free and darted deeper into the wilderness.

Delighted to see hundreds of translucent bubbles floating around the narrow root-rutted trail, Daria knew that the little girl was close by. But what she came across was mind boggling. She entered a clearing in the forest bustling with a village of gnomes, all no more than twelve inches tall. Some were blowing bubbles. Others were sitting upon mushrooms playing games. Three were admiring emerald gems which they hid behind their backs at the sight of Daria.

The gnomes were pudgy, roly-poly, faceless little creatures. Their caps, in a wide array of colors and patterns, were pulled down over their eyes, resting on the tips of their bulbous noses. Their cheeks were covered with scruffy beards that hung over their pot bellies and all the way down to their toes.

The smell of grilled chicken swirled around Daria. She realized she was hungry. Tucked next to a little stream, a few gnomes were wearing long aprons that covered their shirts and bushy beards. They were grilling grubs, snails, and worms on miniature grills. Daria sighed. *I might be hungry, but not that hungry.*

"Pardon me," she said, "I'm looking for a little girl."

"To look is to seek," garbled one gnome through his wiry white mustache.

That's obvious. And uninformative. Not the least bit helpful, Daria thought.

"You seek that which already resides within," a squatty gnome, in an aqua and pink unicorn cap, murmured near Daria's feet. He bobbed his head rapidly to and fro, which sent the pom-pom on the tip of his cap swirling in circles.

"Look within."

"Within," the other gnomes echoed, bobbing their heads in agreement.

"So sorry to say, you misunderstood me," Daria apologized. She positioned her hand about thigh height and asked, "Did you see a girl, about this tall, pass through here?"

"You're tall!" a squeaky voice came from somewhere in the middle of the gnome pack.

"Very tall," a second gnome echoed.

"Tallest I've ever seen!" exclaimed a third.

In what could only be described as the strangest turn of events, several gnomes piled, one atop another, squishing and teetering on the cap below them, until they were Daria's height. The top gnome held the tip of a measuring tape and dropped the other end, letting it unroll to the lowest gnome.

"Ya got it?" asked the top gnome.

"Measure twice. Tallest of all. Giant. Measure twice," prattled the gnome taking Daria's height measurement.

As the towering gnomes tumbled down, Daria felt a pluck at the base of her neck. A gnome in a zigzag patterned cap climbed down from Daria's shoulder, dragging a few strands of her hair. Three gnomes held her strands flat on the ground. They placed a ruler next to it, conferred with each other, then wrote a number on a notepad. Other gnomes measured her shoes and a few sized up the imprints she'd left in the mud. *They certainly are scientific little creatures with an obsession for measurements,* Daria thought.

The gnomes fell silent and stepped away, forming a circle around one of their members. He had a glittery gold cap covered in silver shooting stars. His attire looked like a wizard's. He scribbled on the notepad, examined Daria, then the paper, then Daria. He scribbled again. After a few minutes, he climbed up on a giant mushroom, straightened his cap, and cleared his throat.

The wizard gnome placed his right hand over his chest. He held up the notepad which had numbers scribbled about and checkmarks next to three words: Tall. Long hair. Big feet. He exclaimed in a grizzly voice, "By the power vested from the ancestors of ancient Scandinavian folklore, in the gnome village of Gnomewhere, I hereby and hitherto, indubitably and without a doubt, declare this humanoid... Sasquatch!"

The gnomes jumped up and down, cheering and chanting, "Sasquatch! Sasquatch! Sasquatch!"

Daria stood dumbfounded. Her eye caught sight of one gnome jumping up and down much higher than the rest. Golden curls were sticking out from under the yellow lollipop imprinted cap. *That's her!* The little girl rubbed noses with the gnomes surrounding her and waved goodbye. She did cartwheels into the woodland, leaving her cap laying on the leaf-strewn path. Daria shuffled her feet, pushing through the rollicking gnomes, careful not to trample them.

Daria rounded the bend and the girl was gone. *Nowhere in sight! Again!* Daria was losing faith in actually connecting with her. Standing alone, deep in the dense forest, her heart sank. She didn't know which way to go or which path to traverse. Her feet felt just like her heart, weighted and heavy. Then Daria realized her feet really were getting heavy, sinking deeper and deeper into the ground. Her foundation was unstable. *Quicksand!*

Daria sank until she was stuck mid-waist. *Don't flail. Don't fight it. Most of all, don't panic.* She remembered reading some geek-post about the density of quicksand and the buoyancy of the body making it near impossible to fully sink. Daria was certain the article said "near impossible," and with that she submerged into darkness.

1

SCHLOP! Daria shot out from under the quicksand with a sound like that of canned cranberry sauce when it schlops out of the can. Daria's body splayed across the asphalt ground. The girl with the golden curls was blowing bubbles with her bubblegum just a few feet in front of Daria. She poked a dainty index finger into the bubble, splattering pink goo on her lips, nose, and chin, then ran into the house of mirrors. It was at that moment that Daria noticed she was sitting at the entrance to an amusement park.

Daria entered the hall of mirrors and was immediately bombarded by her reflection. There wasn't a direction she could turn without facing herself. Daria quickly noted her wild head of gray-streaked dingy-brown hair, wrinkled undereye bags, and several dome-shaped nevi speckling her face. As if in slow motion, Daria's face in the mirror stretched sideways, then elongated, and her lips ballooned like a bad Botox injection. To her terror, her face distorted further into the likeness of a creepy clown. She clenched her eyes tight. *Oh, how I hate clowns!* She feared to reopen her eyes.

That fear was justified. Clowns were in every mirror: ghostly white faces, humongous red lips torqued in sardonic grins, bloodshot eyes rimmed with the blackness of death. Their evil laughter rang out from their ecru-yellowed teeth as they mocked her, "You call yourself an author?" "You think you're as creative as they are?"

Daria tucked her head low, petrified to look at the clowns. She maneuvered through the maze of mirrors, bumping into them with every step. *Don't listen to them,* Daria repeatedly thought to herself.

The demons laughed, "You will fail. Doubt is your demise."

Around the next bend, puppet clowns came dangling down from the ceiling, their oversized plastic red shoes bopping Daria on the head. "You care too much what others think." Puppet strings tangled around each other, jumbling them into a knotted mess.

The clowns in the mirrors came to life, peeling off the reflective surface like thin sheets of wallpaper. The paper-thin clowns draped downward toward the floor, then to Daria's sheer horror, they popped up into ghoulishly large 3-D monsters.

Daria crouched into a corner. She hid her head between her knees. *Help me! Please!* And with that, a trap door opened. Daria tumbled down a steep incline, ending in a dusty tunnel.

At least for now, Daria was hopeful that the clowns were gone. Bringing more hope was a thin ray of sunlight glistening through the thick dust at the other end of the tunnel. A flash of movement startled Daria, her eyes widening then squinting to adjust to the darkness. She was sure the girl was standing nearby ready to help her. The girl opened a door to the outside, flooding the tunnel with sunlight.

Daria rushed toward the opening, but soon realized it wasn't going to be as easy as she'd hoped. The cement securing the cobblestone floor was crumbling, twisting her ankles sideways. She fell to the floor. *Be brave!* Daria motivated herself to stand and push forward without hesitation, for she had an eerie feeling that something horrid lurked above.

Cement gargoyles were perched high up on Ionic column pedestals. The gargoyles, putrid puce in color, with bulging eyes and snarling fangs, lined the path to her freedom. One pedestal burst. Then another. Cement shards and powdered dust showered Daria. It only took one quick glance for her to realize that the gargoyles were breaking free from their perches. One massive gargoyle swooped down. Cobwebs draped its face like the drool of a rabid dog. It released a harrowing growl that reverberated, shaking the tunnel walls. The gargoyle's claws were outstretched mere millimeters from piercing Daria's shoulders...

Daria felt the weight on her shoulder and jumped up out of her chair.

"Sorry to startle you," Camille sweetly whispered. "Everyone else already went to the pavilion for lunch."

Daria whipped around to catch her bearings, her voice unable to utter a syllable and her heart pounding beyond her chest. Sunlight was beaming in from the double glass doors on the other side of the room. She saw tables with laptops, coffee mugs, papers, and books strewn about. Cardigan sweaters and throw blankets were haphazardly draped over chairs. Embers from the fireplace's charred wood crackled its familiar popping song. The snack table had been well loved by hungry authors.

Daria looked at the sodalite and labradorite crystals beside her keyboard. Her turtle mug, candle, and giraffe were just where she'd placed them. But her pens were scattered in disarray. The index cards on the desk contained elaborate doodles of intertwining ivy vines, gnomes, clowns, gargoyles... and lessons:

Look within
Not all facts lead to truth
Faith will keep you afloat

Believe in yourself
Face your fears
The only way out is through
Trust your muse

Her knees weakened as she gazed at the cards. Her shaky fingers forged through her knotted hair. She whipped it into a messy bun.

"Writing retreats are enlightening and magical," Camille cooed, unsure of what else to say or do.

Daria nodded. She pulled her burgundy and beige woven shawl tight over her shoulders. She walked with Camille toward the pavilion. While taking deep refreshing breaths of the warm afternoon air, Daria caught a glimpse of the girl with the golden curls skipping in the open field. The child had a gratified glint in her eyes. With each skip, she floated further off the ground. Her silky curls bobbed longer and longer until they were luscious billowing waves. The locks morphed into slotted feathers, like that of an eagle's wings. With a strong but elegant flap, the blowing locks glided her upward. She disappeared into the marbled clouds.

Daria pulled a blank index card out of her pocket. She wrote:

Let your imagination soar!

And this, Daria thought with giddy excitement, *is only the first day of the retreat. I can't wait to see what stories tomorrow brings.*

CHIAROSCURO STATION

Deborah Hetrick Catanese

When passion morphs
to a namby blob
resembling pity
you know the gig is up,
his pole train losing steam within you
and without,
sparkling dew drops
from a leafy past dispersing,
like eon's dust
from passing rails.

Blurred scenery
of endless gripping fantasies
slowly returns to reality's pinpoint focus
as you pull the red cord
above your window seat,
signaling your desire to get off.

The needlepoint satchel
stuffed full of his scent and his stories
weighs on you,
the three step descent on textured metal stairs
feels shaky, clangy, tentative.

You hold sight on Terra Firma,
the concrete platform below you –
awaiting your fine leather-clad foot
to disembark.

But then – you see a flash
of eternity's sultry dappled light,
as flesh and spirit joined as one.
Your hand lingers on the sloping handrail –
your tactile connection to that glorious ride –
before you let go.

As the train whistle moans, and drifts
like inner voices of regret,
a sharp fullness of air
courses through you.
The bellows of your lungs
lend you fire and steam
and you step down,
sure and steady
onto the chiaroscuro platform
of Fare-Thee-Well.

Saint Ottilia's
School for Proper Ladies

Kimberly Kurth Gray

The rumor among students at St. Ottilia's school was that the convent was haunted. It was said to be none other than Mother Marietta Sebastion, founder of the school and the order in 1860, who roamed the halls. Her love affair with the landowner was discovered, and to hide her sin and avoid scandal, the sisters sealed her behind the wall of the great fireplace in the main entrance. Was it true that if you placed your ear close to the mantel you could still hear her nails scratching against the stones?

Gemma Montgomery didn't want to believe these stories, but nevertheless, had avoided the front entrance of the convent every time she went to her music lessons. That was forty years ago and now her sixtieth birthday was approaching. She had sworn that once graduated from St. Ottilia's she'd never visit again. Yet here she stood at the double doors of the old convent for a high school reunion retreat. This was the last place on earth she wanted to be.

Had she not ended up with her former classmates Michelle and Holly at jury duty six months earlier, she'd never have known about this event. They weren't a bad lot, Holly and Michelle, well at least Gemma hoped they'd outgrown their mischievous ways. She hadn't been friends with them at school but neither was she the target of their poisonous taunts. They, along with Cassie and Gianna, had been a clique of mean girls before the term was popular.

It was mostly pathetic little Peggy Roost who sat in their crosshairs. They menaced and stalked her, bellowing "Piggy Roast" down the halls as she passed. With double-thick lensed glasses, buck teeth, and greasy hair, Peggy didn't even bother to avoid them, only laid herself down as a sacrificial lamb giving other gangly, acne-prone, fuzzy-haired creatures an escape from torment. An all-girls' high school was not for the faint of heart.

Gemma trudged up the walkway, lugging a suitcase behind her, the wheels on it long ago rusted in place. "It's only three nights," she said, a phrase she'd been repeating since the taxi mistakenly dropped her at the school on the main road.

Not one to make a fuss, Gemma hauled her bag from the trunk and trekked down the mile-long driveway. Her feet slid across the ice-covered dirt road and though the trees were bare, the sun seemed to avoid this place. The hill up to the convent was as steep as she remembered. When the weathered white crosses of the nuns' graves were in sight, Gemma knew the convent wasn't much further.

A young man in a silver-blue jacket opened the door before her frozen hand touched the knob. "Welcome to Ottilia's Retreat, your home away from home this weekend."

Gemma blinked. A man in the convent? She recovered quickly and smiled. "I'm here for the... um..."

"You must be Gemma." He handed her a slim leather notebook. "You're the last to arrive. In there," he nodded at the book, "you'll find your room key, an agenda for this weekend, and the appointment time for your massage. There are some added pages for notes. My name is Rocco. Please don't hesitate to let me know if you need anything."

Rocco bowed slightly and walked away, his footsteps lost in the plushness of the carpet. It seemed Rocco was available for anything except assisting with bulky bags.

The convent was converted into a space that could rival any four-star hotel. What must the ghosts of nuns past think of the new accommodations? Were they jealous that their home was now luxurious, filled with modern conveniences that would have made their jobs easier? Or were they indignant that this effortless life did not give you time enough to pray and think of God? She suspected that the nuns would be watching over them, judging, shaking their heads and fingers as they'd done when she was a student.

The fireplace stood to her right. A grand creation of stone and marble with an onyx owl statue on the corner of the mantel. It had always reminded her of the Maltese Falcon. She averted her eyes and kept her distance.

An elevator had been added alongside the sweeping staircase, its marble steps worn with use. How many times had she lumbered down to the basement where the music lessons were held? A shiver overtook her as she remembered the last time she'd seen Sister James Albert. Gemma, late for her piano lesson again, had bolted down the stairs, missing a few and stumbling to the bottom. She hated everything about the lessons—ones her mother insisted on—including the dark passageways to the music room and the elderly Sister James Albert with her pruned face and claw-like hands.

"Is that you?" the old nun had called out as Gemma neared the room, panting and wheezing. Sister James Albert was perched on the bench at the piano, staring at the wall.

"There you are, Sister Carmella," the nun said as Gemma approached her. *"Is it time for dinner?"*

Before Gemma could respond, Sister James Albert fell forward, the piano keys clattering under her weight. Stunned, the young girl didn't know what to do and ran from the convent back to school. Once there, Gemma pretended never to have left the building and went to the office claiming she had cramps. Mrs. Buttons phoned the convent to inform Sister James Albert that her next student would miss the lesson. When the secretary couldn't get a response, she sent the janitor to check on the elderly nun. Gemma shook her head trying to dispel the memory of the days following the nun's death.

As the elevator door began to close, she glimpsed a woman dressed in a habit.

"Sister?" Gemma called out, pressing the button and causing the door to reopen. She peered toward the fireplace as a wisp of black smoke dissolved into the rainbow colors gleaming through the stained-glass windows. "Just a trick of the light," she reassured herself, turning back into the elevator.

Though Gemma had been in the convent frequently, no students were allowed on the second floor. Bright paint and new drapes couldn't dispel the imprint left by the Sisters of St. Ottilia's. The fragrance of incense was still prominent in the air and Gemma was sure if she listened hard enough, she would hear the nuns sing their daily hymns as they went to chapel. The heaviness of their presence led Gemma to hurry into the room, firmly shutting the door behind her. Three nights now seemed a long time to be trapped inside the walls of memories and the convent.

The room was pleasant. On the single bed was a hand-stitched quilt that Gemma was positive had been sewn by the nuns who were known for their needlework. An ottoman and a small slipper chair sat by the window which overlooked what was once the laundry garden. In her school days the girls would giggle at the nuns' undergarments hung on the line. There was a secretary desk made of mahogany in the corner next to the closet. Gemma opened the door and found it held a small lingerie chest, several padded hangers under a shelf, and a few hooks.

The room, she imagined, was much different than the cells they'd been when the nuns resided here. After her case was unpacked and squeezed into the bottom of the closet, Gemma prepared to meet her friends downstairs. Reviewing her outfit in the mirror, she smoothed her skirt and touched up her lipstick. That would have to do. She knew she couldn't compete with the others. A widow's pension only went so far and there were no extras for designer clothes or Botox treatments.

Sunshine peeked through the tall, curved windows leaving long shadows and keeping Gemma feeling off balance as she made her way down the staircase. She could hear the murmur of voices from behind the closed library door. Avoiding the fireplace, she tucked around the stairs and up the hallway. After a moment's pause before opening the door, Gemma was surprised to find the room empty.

"I beg your pardon, Miss."

Gemma jumped at the sound of Rocco's voice.

"The other ladies are on the veranda waiting for you. Shall I bring you a cocktail or a glass of wine?"

Placing a hand to her heart, Gemma said, "A cocktail, please." She followed him out the back and into the garden she'd seen from her room.

Gianna was the first to acknowledge her. "Finally," she said, putting her glass down before folding Gemma into a hug. "We thought maybe you'd taken a nap."

Holly, Michelle, and Cassie gathered around Gemma, each taking turns to hug and kiss her as if they'd always been close friends. A warmness grew inside her. It was nice to have a group where she might now belong. The days had become unending since Derek passed. Their boys were now grown up with lives of their own, ones that seldom included Gemma.

She took the cocktail from Rocco and decided not to worry about calories or alcohol content. Gemma was going to enjoy this weekend. "When will the others arrive?"

The women exchanged glances. "Others?" Gianna asked.

"Yes. I know Rocco said I was the last to arrive, but I thought he meant for this evening. Surely others from our class will be here," Gemma said in between sips of her espresso martini. She hadn't had one of these since her son's wedding three years ago.

"No, this is a special retreat. Just us. I'm sure they'll hold some terrible event at an awful restaurant that will include bringing their loud and equally awful husbands," said Gianna with a wave of her manicured hand. "This is much nicer, quieter, don't you agree?"

"Much nicer," Cassie, Michelle, and Holly parroted.

Gemma sipped her drink and decided she wouldn't think about why she had been invited. This retreat was what she needed to put old fears to rest and contemplate new ways to go forward.

Wine was served with dinner, then brandy with dessert. Instead of reminiscing about their school days, the conversations focused mainly on their achievements. Gemma listened as the others listed awards they'd received for volunteering, the successes of their husbands, the degrees they'd graduated with but never used. Gemma didn't contribute much at all. What could she add? She'd dropped out of college to marry then had two babies right in a row. There was no time to volunteer while she raised her boys. Gemma had to get a job as a salesclerk in a jewelry store to help pay for the boys' Catholic school education. Maybe now she could volunteer or even finish the book she'd started writing in high school.

After the cocktails and wine, Gemma doubted she'd have trouble sleeping. She wasn't used to drinking. Her pillow plumped and snuggled under the quilt; her eyes were barely shut when the bells began. Small chimes like those that rang during communion. Gemma sat up and listened. Maybe it was a ringtone on someone's phone, but the sound seemed to come from the hallway. She slipped out of bed and pressed her ear to the door. The chimes grew louder. Her hand shook as she turned the doorknob and tried to adjust her eyes to the darkness of the hallway. No one was about. The bells stopped. Maybe she should refrain from any more alcohol over the next few days.

Snow droplets clung to the window as morning broke. Gemma was excited to get her first massage and especially pleased to have the number one appointment. It was as if she'd won the grand prize. Rocco led her to a room only a few doors from her own. The room was smaller, painted in a soft shade of blue and the scent of eucalyptus lingered in the air. Gemma undressed and put on the terrycloth wrap provided.

She was taken aback to see the burly man dressed in white. Only her husband had ever seen her undressed or touched her. But something in the shy way he smiled and spoke relaxed her. He introduced himself as Brian and explained he was a massage therapist and had been doing this work for nearly fifteen years. The more he talked, the more at ease Gemma felt.

His hands were warm, and the fragrance of the lotion was a pleasing vanilla. Gemma could get used to this way of life, late *al fresco* lunches, cocktails before dinner, weekly massages. It was now hard to recall the snobby girls Gianna, Cassie, Michelle, and Holly were in school and she was glad to see they'd grown into better people, if not still a little vain. It was nice now to call them friends.

When her appointment was over, Gemma went back to her own room wanting to prolong the tranquil mood by taking a luxurious soak in the claw foot tub. The bathroom steamed up as she added bath salts to the water. This would ease any leftover tension. Twenty minutes later she was ready for a nap.

Gemma wiped the steam from the mirror with her hand. "The better to see you with, my dear," she said. Her smile froze when the words 'Why Did You Leave Me?' appeared scratched into the glass.

As she scrubbed, she knew the words would not leave the mirror or her mind. Gemma threw on a bathrobe and hurried down the hall to the massage room where Brian was coming out with Holly.

"Someone's been in my room," she told them.

"Is anything missing?" Brian asked.

"No, it's…" How could Gemma tell them she believed a dead nun had left her a message? "The mirror. Someone scribbled a message on the bathroom mirror."

Brian led the way with Holly and Gemma close behind. Gemma's insides were shaking like Jell-O in those old commercials. She didn't want to see those words again or remember Sister James Albert's lifeless body.

"Here?" Brian pointed to the now clear mirror. He wiped his large hand over the glass. "I don't see or feel anything. Maybe it was a reflection." He turned and looked at the shelves behind them, but there were only a few decorative bottles.

"I'm sorry," Gemma began. "After the massage I took a hot bath and maybe I fell asleep."

Holly rubbed Gemma's arm. "It's okay. I always feel a bit wobbly after massage. Right, Brian?"

Gemma smiled, relieved that the words were gone, and that Holly didn't seem to think she was crazy. Nevertheless, Gemma was positive about what she'd seen. Words etched in glass don't magically disappear.

There was no chance of a nap now. Instead, she went to the closet to choose a dress. Gemma noticed her clothes had been pushed to one side. The inside of the closet was wallpapered, but the pattern didn't line up. She ran her hand along the seam but noticed no bump or parting of the wall. Still, it was odd her clothes had been moved. Gemma had no valuables with her, only a wedding band that she never removed.

Dinner was once again delicious and accompanied by wine. Gemma sipped hers slowly and refused the refills Rocco offered. Tonight, Gianna insisted on playing a game. Gemma loved games, especially Scrabble. An assortment of butter cookies was served for dessert with both dark and white chocolate sauces for dips. As they drank coffee and ate scrumptious cookies, Gianna left to set up the game.

Gemma headed toward the library, but Cassie stopped her. "Not in there," she said and took Gemma by the hand, "The games are set up in the music room. Well, it's the game room now."

How could she excuse herself from the game? Gemma tried to disentangle her hand from Cassie's grip to no avail. By the time they reached the music room, it was Gemma squeezing Cassie's hand. "Sorry," she said, releasing not only her hand but a breath she'd been holding in. Cassie walked away, flexing her fingers.

The room was lit with numerous candles but somehow darkness still prevailed. Gianna sat at a wooden table where the piano had once been. Thick globs of white wax melted onto a saucer. Brown butcher's paper was spread out with digits and letters of the alphabet written in black marker. The words "YES" and "NO" were spelled out near a coin in the center.

"Come in," Gianna said. Holly, Cassie, and Michelle were already seated.

"What type of game is this?" Gemma asked. It looked like a Ouija board.

"We're having a séance," Gianna grinned. "Now sit down so we can begin."

Gemma studied the faces of a group she'd longed to be a part of while in school. She'd wanted to sit with them in the cafeteria and brush each other's hair while they discussed boys, clothes, and music. With those thoughts, Gemma took the chair closest to Holly.

Gianna began. "Welcome. You are welcome to join us. Spirits who are here, come forth, share your story."

The candles flickered, the table rocked slightly, and a cool breeze passed over Gemma. Everyone jumped as the door slammed shut.

"We ask Sister James Albert to join us," Gianna said, staring directly at Gemma, a slight smirk on her face.

She knows, thought Gemma. Then a shadow appeared from the doorway behind Holly. Gemma gasped as the form came further into the room. A nun dressed in full habit. Sister James Albert was with them.

Gemma's chair crashed to the floor as she stood, her body shaking. She couldn't catch her breath, her heart pounded, and gold flecks appeared before her eyes. Her hand went to her throat, but words refused to form. The women stumbled toward her as Gemma collapsed on the floor.

There was a buzzing, a white noise in her head. She felt hands on her and tried to stir. Gemma's eyes were heavy, and a weight lay on her chest.

"Now, child, just rest." Sister James Albert leaned over her. "It will be fine."

Gemma's eyes opened to find a group of nuns surrounding her.

"'Tis a good thing that Gianna called to me. Troublesome as she is, it got me here in time. Lay still, let them do their work. It's not your time."

Gemma vaguely remembered the paramedics and the ride to the hospital but would never forget the nuns waving her off as she was loaded into the ambulance.

The hospital kept Gemma twenty-four hours for observation. No one came to see her except for Holly who had decided to leave the retreat early. She was thankful that the episode had been brought on by anxiety and not a heart attack. When released, Gemma took a taxi back to the convent. This time she arrived at the front door.

There was only one car in the lot and Rocco was not there to welcome her. Gemma had time in the hospital to consider the events of the previous two days. She'd thought a lot about Sister James Albert, how crippled the woman had been and how there'd been no elevator back then. How had she managed the stairs?

Gemma went to the fireplace and touched the old owl. Stories had circulated about the nuns assisting rum runners during prohibition. Similar owls kept watch at The Owl Bar in the old Belvedere Hotel. One eye of the owl would blink when alcohol was available. This might have been a sign here as well if the nuns truly helped in the scheme. She nudged the statue slightly and heard the mechanics of the wall open.

Gianna stood on the landing of the stairs. "Gemma, I'm so glad to see you. You gave us quite a scare."

"I'm sure," said Gemma stepping away from the fireplace.

Gianna came to her. "What are you doing?"

"I had the most peculiar experience while being revived by the paramedics. Sister James Albert visited me."

That same old smirk returned to Gianna's face, but before she became too pleased with her little trick, Gemma went on. "I know that was Rocco dressed as a nun. You planned that, and the disappearing etched mirror, and the chimes. All of it."

Gemma pushed the owl, and a small door unlatched behind the fireplace.

"I can't believe it," Gianna gasped. "All the stories about the nun behind the wall." She glanced inside the darkened cavern.

Gemma hadn't planned to push her former classmate, but Sister James Albert always told the girls to take an opportunity when it appeared. It was the lightest tap that sent Gianna toppling over. In one motion the owl was back in place and the passageway sealed.

Gemma took her time gathering her belongings before locking the front door behind her. She knew Gianna would find a way out. Eventually.

GOODNIGHT, ROOM

Donna Lucas

Go to your Room
Go to your room and retreat.
Sleep. Dream. Refresh. Reflect.
Rise. Shine. Heal. Repeat.
Go to your room and retreat.
-Mom

Dad and I would stand behind your crib, taking turns to watch you fall asleep, your eyelashes fluttering until coming together in a goodnight kiss. We stayed nearby in case you needed us to pet your thick dark hair or hold your tiny hand.

You, dear daughter, were independent and comfortable in your own space. At eight weeks, you slept through the night under a battery-operated galaxy. Above your crib, a starry mobile eased you to sleep as it chirped out the song of artificial crickets. Your sunshiny nursery was stuffed with bunnies, bears, and dreams. A playful alphabet bordered your pastel yellow walls. Your favorites were "D"- Dog and "L"- Ladybug.

Since those precious nursery slumbers, you helped revamp your bedroom, your haven at home, five times before moving into a college dorm. Each makeover marked the beginning of another stage of growth, a new blossom of you.

On your second birthday, two months before your baby sister was born, it was time to move out of your crib into a full-sized bed. You willingly did this for the baby you already loved. You hauled all your stuffed friends to your big-girl room, blooming with ladybug bedding, border, artwork, and curtains. Mr. Bunny, your favorite fuzzy crib mate, joined you in counting spots on your ladybug throw pillows.

You added your own themed décor, too. You colored garden pictures galore and molded clay into bugs and flowers. You finger-painted paper plates and dotted them with a marker. You were a wing away from giving the baby black freckles before I stopped you. Insisting on decorating your sister, you haloed her with your doll's ladybug headband. You wore your Halloween costume year-round, a hooded cape with attached antennae and red and black-spotted wings.

When you were four, we moved, and you got a new room. You gave up your bugs for ballerinas and purple. You thought you owned purple. Dad painted your walls grape bubblegum and your ceiling soft lilac. Appliquéd dancers spun and pliéd on your pillow shams and quilt. Your first pair of ballet slippers slept on a corner shelf. Mr. Bunny wore a tutu and you tied back his ears in a bun.

At this girly-girl stage, you donned a variety of sparkly crowns and refused to wear pants. You improvised and pulled skirts over your soccer shorts. Your closet overflowed with dresses and colorful tights that you masterfully put on by yourself. You were a dancing rainbow.

Eventually, you traded your tiara for a ball cap, leotards for leggings, and princess gowns for a taekwondo uniform. You kept changing and growing, and there was no magic wand in your dress-up bin to slow down the blinking clock of childhood.

For your ninth birthday, you requested a room facelift. You were all purpled out. Your American Girl Doll named Kanani and a wishlist floral comforter set inspired a luau-themed retreat. Tropical blues and greens splashed your walls like the seas of Hawaii. Mr. Bunny wore a grass skirt and lei, and you and Kanani wore matching jammies. You got a blue betta named Dennis who swam in a wall-mounted fishbowl.

Your turquoise bean bag became your island where you listened to Kidz Bop and conquered Common Core Math. There, you also composed lyrics for your neighborhood band, The Dirt Devils, named after the vacuum cleaner you used as a coat rack.

You pinned photos of your best friends and dogs onto corkboards once covered by penguins, teacup pigs, and unicorns. You proudly displayed your taekwondo belts and the boards you broke in half. Posters of heroes from *The Walking Dead* and *The Hunger Games* protected you from the threat of zombies and ruthless governments.

When you were in seventh grade you bought a loft bed from a neighborhood garage sale. Our neighbor's son had grown out of it and was selling it for some extra college cash. You came home with a jigsaw puzzle, hula hoop, squirrel salt shaker, and a request for a free kitten and a bed. You scored an all-in-one twin loft, complete with a bookcase, desk, full-size trundle, and built-in drawers and storage closet. It was perfect for you who craved more teenage space. You loved the thought of climbing a ladder to your private escape (which did not include a free kitten).

You kept the same tropical walls and floral bedding but removed Mr. Bunny's tattered grass skirt. He went *au naturel* wearing just the green gingham bowtie he was born with. We swapped your growth chart with a full-length mirror and your dress-up bin with trending outfits. You hosted sleepovers with friends who borrowed your latest fashions from mounds of laundry carpeting your floor. They shared with you—like good girlfriends do—leaving behind piles of their style too.

Over the next five years, you retreated to your loft more and more. You spent much of your home time there reading poetry and dystopian novels, scrolling social media, listening to music, and nap, nap, napping. Beyond your foot or arm sticking out from above, we saw much less of you. I resented that loft.

It was your senior year when I suggested updating your room with new furniture. The loft ladder was creaky, the drawers were off track, and the closet door dangled from its hinges. The exhausted loft bed was ready to step down. You agreed, always excited to make over your room.

You asked your sister to help pick out colors and decorations and paint before your new three-piece bedroom set would arrive during Christmas break. You picked a pastel yellow and sage quilt, an elephant grey wall, and an area rug that tied it all together. You framed the National Parks puzzle we built, set up a glass essential oil diffuser, and hung a shelf with hooks to replace the Dirt Devil coat rack.

What a lovely bedroom. So tastefully mature with simple, elegant decor. What a treat to be able to see your beautiful face, sans that ladder and loft.

But something about the room felt off, incomplete... Did it need curtains? A floor lamp? A wicker hamper? For months I couldn't grasp what was missing. Plants? More pictures? A vacuum cleaner covered with clothes?

It's the April eve before your eighteenth birthday. I open your door to say goodnight. Standing at the threshold of your room, I'm stuck, frozen in your childhood. I'm in a daze, inhaling fragrances from your youth: berry bubble bath, crustless PB&J, sixty-four new crayons. I breathe in a movie reel of memories. Flashes of you crawling, running, swimming, and laughing. Always laughing. Backyard views of you sitting in the sandbox, playing tag, roasting marshmallows, and performing Dirt Devil songs with your band. Hosting pool parties, slumber parties, birthday parties...

I imagine the clock next to your diffuser striking eighteen times. Your eyelashes flutter as you lie there cozily surrounded by throw pillows, a beautiful past, and a hopeful future.

But something is still missing. It's missing right now.

"Where is Mr. Bunny?" I ask.

"That's random," you say but quickly answer, "I put him away in the closet."

"Closet? Oh, my my. Put away? But you rarely put anything away. Don't you need him?"

"No, Mom. Sorry." You pat your hand, inviting me to an empty spot on your bed.

I cross over and crawl in, silent about Mr. Bunny's retirement. Lying next to you, I realize it's been ages since you played make-believe and dress-up with him. He used to wear gowns to be your princess, hospital patient, and Jedi Knight.

Soon you'll wear a graduation gown. Your next room will be in a dorm at mine and Dad's alma mater, two hours away. I stifle my sobs and dam my eyes in your pillow.

You whisper, "Mommy, do you need Mr. Bunny?"

You let me pet your thick dark hair and hold your mighty hand. "No thanks. Not yet."

Cara, our first-born daughter, graduated with high honors from high school in the spring of 2020. The world was reeling due to the COVID-19 pandemic, but she kept her goal to become a nurse. She packed and left for college that fall. Mr. Bunny stayed back, and his fuzzy ears caught a lot of mom-tears. Online classes, social distancing, and current and future fears made for a uniquely challenging freshman year. Despite it all, Cara persevered, found her support system at school, and leaned on the one back home. After her extended 2020 Thanksgiving break, she put a surgical mask on Mr. Bunny and moved him into her dorm room.

Cara graduated cum laude in the spring of 2024, earning her Bachelor of Science in Nursing. She moved back home and loves being a registered nurse in a local hospital. I'm proud and humbled by her service to others during her twelve-hour night shifts. At the time of writing, she has forty more sleeps in her room until she moves into her own apartment. She has the tools to create a room in which she'll retreat: *Sleep. Dream. Refresh. Reflect. Rise. Shine. Heal. Repeat.*

Goodnight, Room.

MYSTICAL MAYHEM AT THE MONASTERY

Michele Savaunah Zirkle

Here I was for the sixth time, jogging the gravel path at the Mepkin Abbey monastery in the South Carolina heat, praying as hard as it was raining. Praying that mom would be awake by the time I got back so I could eat breakfast. Praying I could keep the food down. Praying that this visit would spark a joy for life I seemed to have lost through divorce decrees and accumulated enemies of the heart.

No one understands me, I thought. *How could they?* I'm oddly mobile. Always on the run. House-hopping. Couch-surfing, I believe they call it now. There's even a website to find a couch if you don't have enough friends who own one, although I do. I'm blessed with amazing friends and family. I'm a nomad, they say. As flighty as the wind, according to my late grandfather—wanting to settle down, but not knowing where. Not knowing how.

My first house, first husband, first child just fell into my open arms. I received the gift of stability and love from my decisions without knowing I was the one whirling the creative lasso. But what's a middle-aged lady to do when she doesn't know in which direction to go and whether to fly or drive or walk to get there?

I'd crawl through a field of stinging ants if one of the monks here could tell me a destination—a physical place

69

where I could reside and be content. Somewhere with enough social events that I don't feel isolated and enough nature trails that serenity is a doorstep away.

As I rounded the bend by the labyrinth, welcoming giant oak trees deflected a bit of the rain. Maybe later when the sun comes out I would walk the circular pattern of goldenrods until I could wring a revelation from God's fingertips. My mind was going in circles anyway. My body may as well follow.

I huffed along the roofed outdoor L-shaped corridor of the first eight rooms, passing the breezeway where a single, lonely hammock swayed. Each of the sixteen rooms housed one individual, each one here for their own reasons, each seeking to squeeze an answer of some sort from this holy place that was once a plantation.

I knocked on mom's door and still no answer. I popped into my adjacent room, showered and knocked again. No answer. I'd told her breakfast was 7:00-8:30. I couldn't imagine her strolling the grounds by herself when she'd never been here before, but I strutted through the parking lot, rain-drenched and sweaty, down the wooden walkway to where I hoped to find her and a hard-boiled egg.

No mom or eggs of any sort awaited me. Just pepper jelly, gluten bread and smiling, nodding strangers. The refectory, Latin for "restore," was a no-talking zone with cafeteria-style tables and a kitchenette. I snagged a scoop of jelly and headed back.

Quiet cultivates deep listening to our inner knowing and connection to the Source that guides us. That's the theory anyway, and I do believe it. I've attended several silent retreats over the years. I've experienced unseen guidance that didn't make sense at the time, yet transformed a life situation into a joyful, new perspective. But right then I was only hearing the chickadees chirping and my soul that was screaming for decisions to be made.

When you can be anywhere, it's hard to know where to be.

Just then an acorn smacked the ground beside me and I heard, "Home is where you are."

The faceless voice was one I hadn't heard in months. Excitement tingled inside my belly. I was hearing again. Answers swelled in the energetic space around me, ready to shower me with direction any moment. Now, if I could just find mom.

I banged on her door. I called her cell. No answer. I was frustrated. A handsome man stepped out of the room a few doors down. He wasn't wearing a lanyard indicating he wished to remain in silence, so I said, "Mom's driving me crazy. Won't answer."

He laughed, his eye twitching. "Maybe she thinks the monks are out to get her."

I made a popping sound with my lips. "I'm going to see to it they do after the morning I've had."

I waved bye and ran around the building to the backside where the windows rose as tall as redwood trees. Peeking into the slit in the curtain, I saw the bed was unmade. No movement. She could be dead. Then I'd feel guilty for getting mad. I pounded on the window. No response.

I showered and slid a map under mom's door with a big, red "X" to show where I'd be when she decided to join the living. I hoped I wasn't being too sarcastic with the universe. Mom and I'd developed a close relationship the past five years that helped to mend the many years she wasn't a part of my life. Not the proms or wedding. Not the boys when they were babies. But she's paid with loneliness and there may be no higher cost to not advocating for yourself than that.

Her decision not to divorce her second husband had haunted her. I didn't want my decision *to* divorce mine to haunt me. Unlike me, she'd been too afraid to leave her dysfunctional marriage. I was the trailblazer, courageous, she'd say. Wished she could've been more like me— independent and self-confident.

The raindrops sunbathed on the grass along the corridor, the chickadees chirped, and I felt the sunrays or the sacred space, or both, were percolating hope in my cells. The warm breeze blew me into the Asian-styled retreat center where clean lines and wood complimented the soft palette. The wall-sized windows framed a spectacular view of the gently sloping lawn full of Magnolia trees and a few birdhouses. The groundskeeper was mowing, the sound lulling me into meditation.

How I wished I could fly. In my dreams I remember how. It's a lot like how Mary Poppins explains it— *"Think happy thoughts."* After years of studying the energy body and metaphysical healing, I realize that flying is often symbolic of wanting to see a broader perspective or to escape. I wanted both.

I wanted to write and teach, but not in a high school classroom like I had for twenty-five years. I wanted to share the skills I've learned and used to manifest substantial change in my life. I wanted to stop being afraid of not being perfect or profound enough to be the example.

I wanted to feel inspired about where to live. I wanted my things out of the storage unit where they'd been for a year. I wanted to have an external home base while I fostered my internal soul home.

I heard the secretary answer the phone and I snapped out of the world of longing. A young lady sat to the right of the shelves stacked with books and swiped her fingers through a tiny sand labyrinth. Maybe the only way to the middle of this Tootsie Pop life really was to walk in circles. Round and round, licking or crawling your way to the core solution—if there even is one.

I poured a coffee, sauntered to the window and stared into the stucco chapel nestled in the horseshoe-shaped yard connecting the retreat center to the rooms. A man knelt in prayer inside.

My mind wandered. Other than the prayer that was uniquely our own, was there a difference between where he prayed and where I did? *No*, I told myself. All prayers are heard.

I prayed for my confusion and worry to subside. I invoked my angels to clear the way for me to surrender to the promptings of my writer's heart. I expressed that I wanted to spend every moment doing what I love, inspiring others to transform their lives, to persevere and to engage the spiritual realms for help. I wanted a place to call home, and I knew that all this required me to surrender to a higher power and let go of the outcome.

"Find her?" A voice snapped me into the moment.

My handsome neighbor settled into a chair and bit into an apple. No wedding ring. I'd take a nibble off an apple from his tree anytime.

"Nope," I said.

"Surrendering to what is helps me when I get stressed," the man said. "Retreat. Interesting that it means both to rest and to withdraw from danger."

I was still processing the word "surrender" being confirmed so soon after my prayer.

"Interesting," I said, hoping I sounded intelligent and not rude, "that this town, Moncks Corner, isn't named after the monks here, but after the person who founded the town."

I sat opposite him on the couch. "I guess the outside world does feel a bit scary. Hadn't thought about a retreat that way, and I've been to so many, my friends call me the Retreat Queen. Ireland spiritual one, shamanic training, energy healing, Hare Krishna kirtans, various ceremonial ones, writers retreats."

"Did you get what you wanted from them?" he asked, his blue eyes genuinely curious.

I drew in a deep breath and a long view through the window of a plane bound north—the direction of the inner warrior. My warrior was worn out. *That's why I'm here*, I silently reminded myself. "I know better than to want anything from them," I said. "Human nature to seek outcome though... so, yes. I left all of them feeling happier, more satisfied with the unknown tributaries of life's current."

"Eloquent. You a writer?"

My insides smiled, and it spread to my face.

"I am. And thank you for evoking that spark that lights up when I even think about writing."

"I'm Owen," he said. His eye twitched, and I wondered if he was trying to wink at me or if he had a neurological disorder.

"Michele," I said. "No bell. Just one L."

"Noted," he said, rubbing the eye and sighing.

"Mine used to do that sometimes. Legs too. You know what's causing yours?"

He shrugged. The eyelid appeared normal now. "I wish," he said.

"Insufficient magnesium maybe?" I offered. I shared my experience with restless leg syndrome and how magnesium intake should be half of the amount of calcium to stay regulated. "I never get twitches anymore."

Owen thanked me. "I'll try those supplements," he said. "Balance in everything seems to be the key."

I stood and winked, instantly wishing I hadn't. "It's almost ten. Better see if I can rouse mom."

I had to pee so I scurried into my room first and was just sitting on the commode seat when I heard a lady's voice from the bedroom side of the partially open wall.

"Hellooo?"

It hit me as I scanned the products lining the vanity. Nothing looked familiar. They weren't mine. I yanked my pants up, stuttered out a sorry and ran out the door.

She sounded like the woman I'd met the previous night as I unpacked the car. I hoped she didn't recognize my voice and was glad she hadn't seen my rear.

I popped into my bathroom and then banged on mom's back window again. This time I yelled, "Let me in!" I felt like the wolf threatening to blow down the piggie's home.

The curtain cracked open and one eyeball peered through the space.

"Mom!" I said, jabbing my finger onto the glass between us. "Open the door."

I scurried to the front as she was opening the door to her dimly lit room. I stepped in and switched on the light.

Mom looked like she'd ridden a roller coaster for the first time. Her dark hair splayed out like sun rays in all directions. Her eyes practically glowed like a wild animal at night.

"You just get up? Didn't you hear me knocking?" I said, waving my hands through the air as if I could coax the mystery from her.

"That was you?" she asked, plopping onto the crumpled bed.

I stared at her in disbelief. "Mom, of course it was me. Who else would it be?"

She burst out laughing.

"You don't know anyone here. You asked me to wake you at seven for breakfast. I've knocked so much my knuckles are sore. Even on the window."

Tears rolled down mom's cheeks as she laughed. An "Oh," would escape every few breaths.

Finally, she said, "I didn't answer because I thought they came to get me."

Her eyes were earnest. Was she totally losing it? Maybe she was as crazy as she looked.

"Who?"

"The monks," she squeaked out.

I shook my head. "The monks? What in the world would monks want with you?"

The bed shook with her laughter.

I stood laughing with her. Not making any sense of it, just laughing at the absurdity of her being afraid of monks and that the cute stranger next door had pegged it right.

After several rounds of laughter, her stopping, me starting, our laughter conversation like a comedic waterfall, we resumed a fairly normal breathing pattern so we could talk.

Mom tucked her chin and peered up like a child. "I thought they wanted me to go to church."

"Church?"

"Yes, church," she said, eyebrows raised and mouth gasping for air through the laughs.

"That's absurd!" I said. I flung my arms out wide. "My God, Mom, I told you that you don't have to do anything here you don't want to do. No services. No nothing."

"I forgot, but I wasn't going." She blew her slightly elevated nose and wiped her eyes with her sleeve. "You taught me well. Getting more like you every day."

"Progress! Sticking up for yourself," I said. "I am a good coach!" If I could help her, maybe my life coaching *could* help others.

"Get dressed," I told her. "We're taking a walk and believe me, the mosquitoes are scarier than the monks."

The trees bulging with moss and the azaleas pregnant with blooms rendered a serene, fantasy-like quality to the tombstone-lined, gravel path leading to the Cooper River where Henry Laurens, former owner of the plantation and founder of the first multimedia company, including *Time* and *Life* magazines, was cremated.

Mom and I walked past the alligator pond where the creature swam, his scaly back barely breaking the surface, and stepped through the open gate at the Laurens' family cemetery.

"Cool trivia. The first cremation in the United States happened here." I pointed to the stone where Henry's skull was buried. "Henry was petrified to be buried alive like he had almost done to his little girl. She'd been declared dead and placed near an open window. This was the custom so her soul could easily depart. Anyway, the mist from a rain stirred her, and those sitting with her saw she was breathing."

"How awful!" Mom said. She cleared her throat and gulped water from her thermos.

"Oh, that's not all. After Henry's body was set fire on a funeral pyre, legend has it his blazing head rolled into the river," I said, pointing to the river visible beyond the bluff, "and had to be retrieved by a slave so his skull could be buried right here. Lots of folks were scared of being buried alive back then, so they started putting bells inside caskets so if someone was alive inside they could ring it. That's where we get the saying, 'Saved by the bell.'"

"What a story to start my day with," Mom said, looking to the sky.

I pointed to a landscaped field down the path. "A slave cemetery over there—for the few that have a headstone. The rest are buried throughout the grounds."

"I know one thing. Life's short and I'd never live with a controlling man again, let alone marry one." She shook her head, a few gray strands glistening like a crown in her black updo. "He had to die before I realized how badly I needed to escape. Never again. I'm free," she said, looking heavenward. "Just like the slaves who tilled this ground. Free in this world or the next." And with that, she walked out the gate.

I followed and poked her shoulder. "Won't be long until someone will be saying, 'Alas, poor Yorick' about us." Mom's scrunched up face prompted me to explain. "He was a Shakespeare character whose skull was found by his friend, Horatio, a gravedigger. He grieved the death and said, 'I knew him, where is his song now?'"

"Halleluiah!" Mom said. "That's my song. So let's enjoy this gorgeous day."

We strolled toward the river where boats buzzed by creating a trail of foam and swirling water and sometimes pulling a skier. The whimsical scene was refreshing.

"Watch out—a monk!" I yelled and jumped to the side, startling mom who stopped dead in her tracks. Then scanning the lawn empty of monks and noticing my smile, she said, "Funny."

"You're usually the one scaring the shit out of me," I said. "That time at Francie's when I'd went to the bathroom at midnight knowing you were asleep in Francie's room." I shook my head. "And came in to find you sitting in my bed. I swear, I thought *The Exorcist* girl had gotten me! Your hair was wild like this morning and that mannequin in the corner and that spooky canopy draped over the bed didn't help anything."

Tears of laughter were already grazing mom's face.

"That was the best," she choked out, keeping stride with me. "The look on your face."

"Almost beats me peeing in a stranger's bathroom this morning," I said.

Mom stared at me as we reached a bench perched on the hill overlooking the pearl blue river.

"Yep, walked right into the room on the other side of mine. Was in a hurry. At least it was a woman's room. She yelled from the bedroom side. Between you and her... quite the exciting morning."

We cozied onto the bench fortressed by the sun-teased treetops. The dragonflies darted low atop the freshly mown lawn while bells rang in the distance marking the remembrance of all those who'd worked the land and who were buried there.

I decided to be more like the dragonflies. They fly backwards as easily as they do forward. I could revisit the past quickly when I need to work with a feeling but don't have to get stuck there.

I accepted the deep realization that the answers I seek are already with me, just like mom was in her room all along. I embraced the idea that I don't need an international airport or a best-seller sitting on a shelf in one in order to be happy. I don't even need to settle down and buy or rent a house. I just need to be as present in the moment as I can and be still enough to hear my heart-inspired guidance.

I laid my arm around mom's shoulder. "I'm glad you got to come with me this time. I'm going to go into silence after dinner and we'll see how long I can last. Only two days to go."

"You have discipline. Michele, my bell," she sing-songed.

I smiled. "At least I'm not ringing from inside a casket." I squeezed her shoulders tight. "You know you're the only one I let call me that, except Grandma when she was living."

"She'd be so happy we reunited. No man will ever come between me and my girls again." Mom patted my hand. "Maybe your sister can come along next time."

And with that I allowed the past to dissolve like the rain from the morning's shower.

Watching the strawberry sunset fade to orange that evening from the bench, a few scattered pilgrims finding a spot to stand or sit and see the spectacular light of hope for whatever they'd come there to work out or work on, I felt inspired to breathe deeply, purposely, for if anyone had mistaken me for dead, I'd ring the bell so loudly Big Ben would be jealous.

I thought about what Owen had asked about my take-away from various retreats.

I knew that at retreats a centrifugal force in my belly drew me into myself, my desires, my longings, in a way that I didn't tap into on my own as often as I need to.

I knew they stimulated a renewed sense of self, whether walking the Oregon Coast, ferrying to the Aran Islands or tapping away at the writers lodge in Pennsylvania. I was the coordinating factor. I was the key to my own resetting, rejuvenating and reinventing. I was the retreat center.

I had everything I needed and more. I loved myself, and I was the best lover I could ever have.

I still felt all fuzzy inside when an intriguing man with an eye twitch tapped me on the shoulder while the Cooper River glistened as far as the eye could see.

ON THE CORNER OF GULL WAY
AND ROBIN DRIVE

Amy Morley

I spent several days
throughout the months of
May, June,
and July

on the
Eastern Shore in

Delaware, Maryland,
and Virginia

driving up and down this
coastal peninsula
known to the world as Delmarva.

This peninsula known to me
was my retreat
to a grieve leave in a seaside town

of sea cove wonders,
fantastical nuggles, and ospreys
who gave me
his triton, Roses, a pomegranate tree, and
guided Fishie back home to their Queen

when they arrived together
in honor of me
on the corner of Gull Way and Robin Drive.

Over the course of three months' time
something haunted me through the coastal breeze
on a journey that brought
eternal peace.

WINE DOWN WEEKEND

Lisa Valli

It only took ten years to get her degree, and Taylor was finally ready to celebrate with the two people who meant the most to her in the world. She wheeled the Jeep Wrangler up the sprawling drive of the Pinecrest Inn. Despite her upbringing nearby, she was a first-time visitor to this part of Pennsylvania. She parked in front of the entrance and spotted the valet waiting there in the blistering July sun.

She unfolded all five foot eleven inches of herself out of the front seat and tossed her keys to the young man.

"Excuse me, ma'am. Do you have any bags?"

From the back seat, she retrieved a blue, faded duffle that matched her flared denim jeans and plopped the black fedora on her head.

"I got it," she called back, entering the building through ornate double doors.

The lobby was magnificent, with a dark mahogany staircase curving down on both sides of the entryway. In between two coffee-colored leather couches sat a glass coffee table. Plush wing chairs upholstered in rich ivory damask flanked the couches. A carved cherry bar was situated on the side of the room, its scent of furniture polish rich in the air. It gleamed from the chandelier above.

She strolled over to the reception desk and waited for someone to check her in.

After a few minutes, she leaned up over the desk, craning her neck to see into the room behind the reception area.

A throat clearing behind her, "Ahem," made her whirl around to discover a tall, handsome man. "Can I be of assistance?" he asked in a deep voice imbued with a sexy British accent.

She smiled, looking up at him, dumbstruck for a second. He was a good head taller than her.

"Hi there," she said, extending her hand. "I'm here to check in. Is anyone around to help me with that?"

Shaking her hand, his larger one covering hers, his brown eyes met her blue ones.

"Yes, let me get someone to help," he said as he turned away. He then turned back to her, saying, "By the way— I'm Max. Are you here for the Wine Weekend retreat?"

"Yes, I am. My name is Taylor." She smiled.

"It's a pleasure to meet you, Taylor. I'm the sommelier. I'll be running the tasting programs this weekend. Glad you could make it. Let me find someone to help you right away."

Her gaze followed him as he went around the corner. A minute later, he was behind the desk facing her.

Raising an eyebrow, she said, "I thought you were the sommelier."

"I am," he chuckled. His smile lit up his face and his eyes crinkled at the corners.

Oh gosh! He's so damn cute.

"The owner is out on the veranda setting things up for the cocktail party tonight. I told him I could help out in here. What's your last name, Taylor?"

"Vincennes with three N's."

He clicked on the keys and said, "Okay. I found you. Do you have a driver's license and credit card for incidentals?"

"Sure," she said, rifling through her bag.

"Taylor!" a high-pitched voice called out from behind her.

Taylor spun around to see her high school friend Emily rushing toward her.

"Emmie!" They hugged each other, laughing at the same time.

Taylor pulled back to get a good look at her friend. "You look great! And I'm glad we were able to get this in before you got pregnant... again!"

Emily laughed. "I'm done. Three is enough!"

They hugged again and Taylor turned back to Max.

"This is the second person in our party. Emily Michaels."

"Got it," he said as he typed again into the computer. "And you have one more, correct?"

"Yes. And she is here as well," a female voice called from the entranceway.

Emily turned around and yelled, "Samantha! You made it! All the way from D.C."

"Virginia, actually." Samantha sauntered across the room, her black, alligator Louboutins click-clacking on the lobby floor. The black suit she wore hugged her body and the crisp white blouse didn't look like it had one wrinkle, even after three hours in the car.

"It's fabulous to see you." She embraced both of her friends at the same time.

Emily said, "You look great! It seems like forever since we were together."

Samantha rolled her eyes, "Emmie, it was a year ago."

"I know. But it's still too long for me," she said feigning a sad face.

Taylor turned back to Max once again. "And this is Dr. Samantha Pryor. Ladies, this is Max. He is our sommelier and wine guide for the weekend."

"Hi, Max!" Emily and Samantha said together in a sing-song voice.

"Such a pleasure to meet you," added Samantha.

Max said, "The pleasure is all mine. Now, if I can get a driver's license and credit card from each of you, I will get you all checked in. We have you in Room 10, the family suite. There are two bedrooms. One has a king bed, and the other room has two full size beds. Here are your key cards and the schedule for the weekend activities. The welcome party starts tonight at 7:00 PM on the veranda which is just through these doors over here to the left." He motioned to the side entrance. "We will be tasting various wines and there will be complimentary appetizers as well. If you wish to reserve a table for dinner tonight in our dining room, just let me know and I can do that for you."

"Yes. I believe we'll want to make a reservation. How long do you expect the welcome party to last?" asked Samantha.

"I think you would be safe if you made a reservation for 8:15 or any time afterwards."

"8:15 is fine," Samantha said without asking her friends. "Alright. Let's get this weekend started," she said and rolled her bag to the elevator.

The living room in the suite was lovely with a soft cushy couch, a plush rug, and a couple of chairs near a stone fireplace. Not that they would need that this time of year, but it was something to keep in mind for wintertime if they decided to come back.

For the past ten years they had gotten together almost annually. The retreats had included yoga weekends, culinary sessions, book lovers retreats and even a silent retreat, which they found to be too challenging and decided never to do that one again.

Samantha, the self-appointed leader of the group, typically searched out the retreats and emailed the others for their approval. But Taylor had found this one. Somehow a weekend of learning about wine and relaxing with a nice Bordeaux resonated with her right now. And the others had agreed. She was embarking on a new chapter in her life and she was really looking forward to it.

Samantha took the room with the king bed. As an M.D. she made more money and contributed more to the cost than the other two. Especially Emily who had been a stay-at-home mom the last nine years.

"C'mon, girls! You ready to go downstairs? We're already fifteen minutes late," Taylor called from the living room. The other two were still primping and posing in their respective bathrooms.

"Yes, I'm ready." Emily walked out straightening her skirt and fidgeting with her top. "Everything is so tight these days. I need to buy some new clothes. But I never have any time!" she wailed.

Samantha walked out, looking perfect in a green cocktail dress that highlighted her honey gold hair and sea green eyes. "Oh, Emily, come on. You've got time for shopping. You don't have a job."

Emily turned toward her with a scowl on her face. "Excuse me. I've got three little ones at home all under age six. That is more than a full-time job!"

"I just meant your schedule is more flexible than ours. Taylor had classes during the day and bartends at night. I'm booked every day with patients."

Emily looked at her wide-eyed. "You have no idea what it's like, Sam. I'm running from the moment I get up until I fall into bed at night. And I'm tired the whole day long. It's harder than anything I've ever done."

"Okay. Sorry, I didn't mean to rain on your parade."

"Let's go!" said Taylor, rising from the couch. Wearing an aqua dress with dark strappy sandals, she towered over both of them. Tall and statuesque, she looked like a Viking princess, blonde hair and blue eyes shining.

Downstairs they walked out to the veranda which opened onto a sprawling green lawn. High top tables with white tablecloths and votive candles graced the porch. All the guests were on the lawn surrounding a large round table.

Max was in the center of the group lifting up a glass of white wine, asking everyone to inspect it.

When the three women approached, Max said, "Ladies, welcome! Everyone, this is Taylor, Samantha, and Emily. We are just starting our intro into tasting." Then looking back at his glass, he said, "The five things to focus on when you taste wine are sight, smell, swirl, sip and savor."

He held the glass up higher for everyone to see and then swirled it. He brought it to his nose and sniffed and then went in for the sip. He closed his eyes and held the wine in his mouth for a second and then swallowed. Taylor let out a giggle. She couldn't help herself. She remembered once when she was bartending, a man doing these five actions in a very exaggerated way to impress his girlfriend. Max shot her a quick glare while he pointed to everyone's glasses in front of them.

"Now I want you all to try it." Then glancing back at her, he said, "And you too if it's not too much trouble."

Taylor blushed. "Oh no. Sorry. I was just thinking of something from—"

"What we are tasting here, folks, is a Pinot Grigio," he continued. "It's a subtle, soft, and approachable wine with a mild, fruity flavor. It's a good wine to start with since it's light with low tannins and moderate acidity. We want to keep your palate clear as we move onto more full-bodied wines." He stole another glance at her before picking up the next bottle on the table.

Later as the ladies stood around one of the high tops munching on baked feta bites and crab stuffed mushrooms, Samantha raised her glass and said, "I'd like to make a toast to Taylor who graduated with honors in Art History. I know it took a lot longer than you thought, but you did it!"

"To Taylor!" Emily chimed in.

"Thanks, guys," said Taylor taking a sip. "It took me a long time to decide what I wanted to do. And dropping out nine years ago didn't help things. But I got back on track and followed the dream. Now I just have to find a job," she winked.

"You will! No doubt," Emily said. "But I do have to say, Taylor, I think you really ticked off the sommelier."

"Ugh! I didn't mean to. I was thinking of one of my customers and it made me laugh. I didn't intend to be rude. But hey, the guy's gotta chill. I mean, we're all here to relax, right?" she said lightly as she took a sip of a smooth Pinot Noir. But her eyes darted around looking for any sign of Max. She needed to apologize.

"Well, all I can say is, he couldn't take his eyes off of you the whole evening." Samantha nibbled on a mushroom. "I don't know about you two, but I don't have much room for dinner."

"Let's just get a salad. I heard the dining room is beautiful, and I can't wait to see it," Emily said.

"You don't get out much, do you Em?" Samantha laughed. "Okay, let's go. It's almost time for our reservation."

Taylor gave Samantha a disapproving glance behind Emily's back, but she was already walking ahead of them toward the dining room.

After dinner they headed out to the lobby bar where a lot of people from the tasting earlier had gathered. They each ordered an after-dinner cocktail and listened as the others discussed the upcoming activities.

"I can't wait for the dinner tomorrow night with the wine pairings. I did it last year and the food was spectacular," said a woman who was standing at the bar. "I couldn't see straight by the time dessert came."

Her husband put his arm around her and snickered, "I sure enjoyed it too honey." He kissed her cheek.

"John would love this place," said Emily as she watched the couple. "I'll have to bring him here."

"If you have the time," Samantha chirped.

Taylor whirled around to look at her. "What is going on with you? Why are you so snippy!"

Emily looked up at Taylor as if to shut her up.

Samantha returned Taylor's glare. "I don't know what you're talking about."

"You don't? Well—"

"Taylor. It's okay," Emily interrupted.

"No, it's not, Em," Taylor said casting her a sympathetic look. "Sam has been on you ever since we got here."

"Ugh. Okay. Sorry if I've been, what did you call it? Snippy? I apologize," Samantha said in a haughty voice.

Taylor put down her aperitif and said, "I'm heading upstairs. Em, are you coming?"

Emily put down her drink and followed Taylor. Samantha leaned back against the bar and took a long sip from her drink.

The next morning, they got ready for Brunch with Bubbles. Samantha had woken up early and attended the 9:00 AM yoga session and was now in the shower.

"This should be fun," said Emily, her brown eyes shining. "Champagne and omelets. You can't beat that!"

"I want to be on time today. Samantha, how long will you take to get ready?" Taylor called out when she heard the shower turn off.

"Thirty minutes," came the response.

"We're going to go down now. We don't want to be late. We'll save you a seat," Taylor said.

"Okay."

When Emily and Taylor arrived at the dining room, the guests were being seated at a long rectangular table. Max was at the head of it, lining up four bottles of sparkling wine. Taylor met his eyes as she sat down near him, giving him her full attention. He smiled at her, and she got a warm feeling inside. She sensed that he'd forgiven her for the outburst yesterday, but she still intended to speak to him about it.

"Good morning, everyone. I trust that you slept well," he started, his British accent sounding stronger this morning, causing Taylor to get goosebumps. He went on to describe the different wines in front of him, telling them that something couldn't be called Champagne unless the grapes were grown in the Champagne region of France.

"This morning, you'll be sampling Prosecco from Italy, Cava from Spain, sparkling wine from the Napa Valley and a Champagne from France." He went on to discuss that sparkling wine is served in narrow-topped flutes to retain the bubbles as he poured a little into everyone's glasses.

When he got to Taylor, he took his time and brushed her hand as he poured. She felt her stomach do a flip-flop. "I'm sorry about yesterday," she whispered. "I didn't mean to interrupt. I moonlight as a bartender, and I was reminded of one of my customers and I laughed. It wasn't directed at you."

"You moonlight as a bartender? Well, maybe you'll have to give me some lessons on cocktail making later," he smiled at her. She nodded a little too eagerly and caught herself.

At that moment Samantha walked in, looking stunning as usual. Honey-gold hair had been brushed until it shone, and her makeup looked like it had been applied by a professional at a Neiman Marcus cosmetics counter.

This is how it had always been, Taylor mused. Samantha, perfectly coiffed, dressed to the nines. Emily, casual, cute, and petite with a beautiful inviting smile. And Taylor, the free spirit born from two former hippies, normally sporting jeans, boots, and a cropped t-shirt.

After they finished the tastings, they sat down for a brunch of Eggs Benedict, Belgian waffles, hickory smoked bacon, fruit salad and baskets of pastries and fresh breads. Samantha suggested they explore the Inn a bit followed by a dip in the pool.

By the time dinner came, they all felt relaxed and refreshed. Taylor came out of the bathroom after her shower, vigorously drying her hair with a towel. "What are you girls wearing tonight?"

"Ugh, I feel so tired," Emily said, lying on the couch. "I don't have the energy. I feel like something's wrong with me."

"You always feel like something's wrong with you," Samantha said.

"What do you mean?" Emily said, an irritated edge to her voice.

"Forget I said anything, Em." Samantha went on brushing her hair in the mirror.

Emily sat up. "No. I want to know what you meant."

"Ever since I've known you, you're always thinking something's wrong with you. You're like my patients who sit on WebMD searching their symptoms and then come to my office with their self-diagnosis. I tell them to stay off the internet," she said with a huff.

"Well excuse me, Dr. Pryor!" Emily shot up from the couch and stomped into her bedroom.

Samantha looked at Taylor who was staring back with her hands on her hips.

"What?" Samantha said. "I just call it like I see it."

"Why are you being so mean to her?" Taylor hissed under her breath.

Samantha rolled her eyes. "I'm not mean to her. What does she have to complain about? She has a husband who loves her. She doesn't have to do the 9-5 like most people do every day. She never had any issues getting pregnant.

I mean, look at her. She's got three kids and she's just over thirty years old."

"Sam, what's this about?"

Samantha looked down at the brush in her hand and shook her head.

Taylor continued. "I'd say you're the one who has it all. You're gorgeous. You're a doctor. You make a ton of money. You're engaged to Chad, a successful investment advisor—"

Samantha looked up quickly and stared straight at her, not saying a word.

Taylor stopped. "What?"

"Nothing."

"Don't say *nothing*. What is it?" Taylor pleaded.

"I'm not engaged anymore," Samantha said, looking at the floor.

"But... what are you talking about? You're wearing your ring." Taylor pointed to the two-carat diamond on Samantha's left hand.

Samantha dropped down into the chair and put her head in her hands. "Chad broke up with me. I was too embarrassed to take off the ring."

"Too embarrassed in front of who? Emily and me?"

Samantha nodded, her head still covered by her hands.

"He said I was too self-absorbed."

Taylor didn't say anything.

Samantha looked at her. "I know. I know... I have been. All during med school, it was always work, study, work, study. I never had time for myself. Now I finally do. I don't want to do anything I don't want to do. I've been doing things for everyone else for so many years!"

"I thought becoming a doctor was something you wanted to do for yourself."

"No," she shook head as tears came to her eyes. "No. It's always been something my parents wanted for me. I'm not sure I even want to be a doctor."

Taylor knelt on the floor in front of her friend, taking Samantha's hands in hers.

"Sam, you are a grownup now. You don't have to do what you don't want to do because of someone else. Maybe you just need a break to figure out what you really want. You spent eleven years in school and then went straight into practice without so much as a vacation. It's a lot."

Samantha squeezed Taylor's hands. "I couldn't wait to come here and see you and Em. You've always been there for me. I needed this."

They both stood up and hugged each other. "Now let's go and see Em," said Samantha. "I need to apologize."

They knocked on Emily's bedroom door which was ajar.

"Come in."

They walked in and realized Emily had been crying.

"I'm so sorry," said Samantha rushing over to the bed.

She sat down on one side, and Taylor sat on the other as Emily looked up at the ceiling.

"I didn't want to say anything to ruin this weekend," she said still staring up. "I found out I have breast cancer," Emily said in a monotone voice.

Sam's eyes widened and Taylor covered her gasp so Emily wouldn't hear it.

"What stage are you? What treatment has been prescribed? Are you on any medication?" Samantha had shifted to doctor mode.

For the next hour, they talked, cried, and hugged, but most of all supported each other as only close friends could do.

"I went to med school with a fabulous oncologist who works at the University of Pittsburgh Medical Center. He has a new cutting-edge treatment for breast cancer, Em. I'm going to call first thing on Monday and get you in to see him." Samantha hugged her and continued, "He's the best. You're going to be alright. I know it."

Emily cried in her embrace and said, "And I will pray that things work out with you and Chad. You two belong together."

"Oh, you heard us talking out there?" Samantha smiled. "We'll see. I think I need to do some work on myself first."

She pulled back and gave a weak smile as she brushed a strand of hair from Emily's face.

"I'm not hungry. I'm going to stay here," said Emily.

"Me neither," added Sam. "I'll stay here with you."

They both looked at Taylor. "That just leaves you," said Samantha.

"Yes, you need to go downstairs and see that British hottie. It's clear to everyone that he's got a thing for you."

"No. I can't leave you two," Taylor said, shaking her head.

"Nonsense. Go get ready. We'll be fine," replied Samantha, her arm around Emily's shoulder.

Fifteen minutes later, Taylor walked to the elevator and pushed the lobby button. She had a feeling she'd be heading back to the Pinecrest Inn by herself in the near future. But for now, she was thankful for her girls and the love they shared for each other.

GREEN THUMB

Melinda Tauler

Carly Green knew very early that she was different, but it took her a while to understand what that really meant. For one thing, she had a way with plants. And not in a normal "green thumb" kind of way. She could speak to them and understand them in ways that other people could not. She didn't realize right away that everybody couldn't do the exact same things that she was able to do— wake the plants up, make them feel better, and truly understand them.

Not only was she able to communicate with plants, she had the same gift with spirits who had recently passed but had not yet moved on to whatever comes next. If she intervened quickly, she could keep them around until she was ready to let them go, which, so far, was never.

It was comforting to have these connections who could never choose to move on from her until she was good and ready for them to do that. And besides, she only collected the spirits whose families didn't show up for them.

When Carly's father embalmed a body that was turned over by the town of Teabrook or the county home and there was no next of kin, Carly felt a certain responsibility to those forgotten people. Everybody deserved to feel cared about, and that's all she was doing—making sure that nobody felt left behind. She wanted anybody who passed on and came through her father's funeral home to have someone looking out for them. The town would pay for a simple burial if a person was alone in the world, but you couldn't really call it a funeral if there was no one in attendance. People in that situation went straight into the ground without any of the ceremony or tears.

Carly learned how to bind spirits from a book she took out of the library at John F. Kennedy High School. It didn't have a code on the spine like all the other books around it. There were weird markings inside its pages, and the cover was made of leather—not exactly the kind of thing you'd expect to find in a public-school library.

Tingling usually escaped through her fingers—she pulled the magic out of herself to help plants when they needed it. This time, that same electric feeling switched direction and moved up her arm when she touched the book, making her feel warm all over like she was glowing from the inside out. There was no checking something like that out of the library, and there was no way she could just leave it there for someone else to find. How would you borrow a library book if it wasn't even in the system? And so, Carly did the only thing that made sense. She looked around to ensure that nobody was watching, and she put it in her bookbag.

According to the book, to bind a spirit, you just had to make your intention known. A drop of blood needed to be put together with the binding object. And then, that spirit would be bound until either the person who set the spell broke it or died. Once the necessary preparations were done, you would chant:

"My friend, my friend, stay close to me. A drop of blood and you'll never leave. We close the circle, two as one. My friend, my friend, you shall not run. You will stay close, you will stay near, my friend, my friend, you are now bound here."

Darker things like learning to bind spirits held a certain appeal for Carly. Enough so, that she started dressing the part, or that's what the other kids at school said. Never to her, of course, but she knew. She heard their hushed whispers in the hallways, and it broke her inside every time it happened. Nobody at school wanted to be friends with the weird girl who talked to plants or dressed like she was already dead, or for that matter, had actual dead bodies in the basement of her house.

Back in elementary school, things were different. Carly had a friend once. Leah used to knock on her door and invite her to go ride bikes. She even came over for a sleepover once. That all changed when Leah got nervous because there was an ambulance outside.

"Oh, that's for Dad. He gets people ready to be buried."

That was the last time Leah came to her house. After that, the whispers in the hallways at school started.

Mom died when Carly was born, so there wasn't any comfort to be found there. Even though Dad tried to help any way that he could, it wasn't the same as having her own friends, so again, she did the only thing she knew to do—she started experimenting with the spells in the book. That binding spell was especially powerful and seemed simple enough to attempt.

Carly had an after-school job at Jed and Dino's Plant Nursery, and it was lucky that her bicycle had a basket on it. If there was a plant that got hurt or wilted, she was supposed to throw it out to keep everything in the nursery looking fresh, but she would sneak them into her bicycle basket and adopt them to join the rest of her plant children instead. This happened enough times that she had quite a collection. She would rather retreat into herself than deal with people who didn't understand her. The family of plants she put together made her feel like she didn't need to do that so much anymore.

The book said that anything could be used as a spirit vessel, and she had lots of plants around. It made sense that her plant babies should be where all the spirits she bound would live. She could connect the souls of lost people to the bodies of unwanted plants and surround herself with beauty and companionship.

It wasn't a long wait before another one of those bodies nobody cared about showed up courtesy of the county home. This was the perfect opportunity to try her new skills with spirit binding.

The lady looked like she might be anybody's grandmother, complete with curly white hair that was almost see-through and a pleasant face. The tag on her toe said her name was Marguerite Henry. When the woman climbed out of her body, Carly knew this was her chance.

"Hello," she said. "I'm Carly."

An unfamiliar, but kind voice said, "I'm Margie. Can I help you, dear? You look nervous."

"Do you think when we go from here, that there's anything afterward, or is it just open space and nothingness?"

"I'm not sure, honey, but there's my body over there, and here I am. I'd like to think there's more, but I just don't know. I was at the salon for my weekly appointment and now I'm here. What do you think?"

"I think there's probably only something there if you believe there is. Otherwise, who knows. Are you scared about what's going to happen now?"

The walls began to feel like they were crushing in. The room started to be more shadow than light. And then, the process of essence migration started. All the love leaked out through every part of Margie that Carly could see. It looked painful to forcibly separate a spirit from a body. It reminded her of when a spider traps a bug in its web and rolls it up tight before sucking all the life out. Margie looked terrified.

She had just come home from the plant nursery and still had that day's rescue in the pocket of her jacket—a cute little pothos that should do nicely if this worked. Carly pulled a safety pin out and pricked her thumb. She had spent enough time with that leather book to have the words memorized.

"I now bind Marguerite Henry to this plant. My friend, my friend, stay close to me. A drop of blood and you'll never leave. We close the circle, two as one. My friend, my friend, you shall not run. You will stay close, you will stay near, my friend, my friend, you are now bound here. Marguerite, you are now bound. You may not leave."

Carly almost couldn't believe it. It worked on the first try. She knew because once the binding was complete, the walls no longer felt like they were pushing in, and the shadows went away.

"Margie? Are you okay?"

"Yes, yes. I'm fine, dear. Thank you for helping me."

"We have got to find you a pot."

And up they went to Carly's room to put Margie in her permanent position near the window.

"Margie?"

"Yes, dear?"

"Margie, do you ever think about what would've happened if I hadn't been fast enough that day?"

"Of course, dear. I think that would have been it for me. It didn't feel like there was any coming back from that."

Carly started keeping a closer eye on the bodies coming in and out of the house. Sometimes the people didn't want to be bound, but she knew better and so did Margie. Whether or not that person could be convinced, they were going to be bound. It was really for the best. Saving them meant that they didn't have to have their essence forced out, and that she had another person to talk to—another friend to add to her collection.

"Pete? Peeeeete! Wake up! Can you help with my homework?"

"Girl, I'm sleepin.' Let old Pete alone. Ever since that day you stopped me from goin' anywhere of my own accord, you haven't ever let me get a wink. All that rest-in-peace garbage sure fell short."

"You could be grateful, you know. Eternal damnation and all that. There's always a chance you could've gone the other way. Be happy you got to skip that part. Besides, you're a ghost now, and ghosts don't need to sleep. Would you please help me?"

"Damn kids. I should never have told you I knew anything at all about math. Always wanting help with your algebra homework and so on. Sure, I can do it, but maybe I don't feel like it. Ever cross your mind? I really thought death would come with a lot less responsibility. You wouldn't think a living person could haunt the dead, but I tell you—it's possible, and here's proof."

"Do you really mean that? You think I'm haunting you? What a mean thing to say, Pete. Maybe you should think of it like a little retreat."

"You can't trap a person in a place without even asking first and then expect them to be happy about it. That's kidnapping, you know. And you have the gall to think I'm gonna be grateful?"

As Carly's collection of friends grew, so did the resentment she felt. After all she'd done to make sure that physical death wasn't spiritual death, you would think a person would be grateful. That was the least she expected. But no, a lot of times they couldn't even be bothered. She had to admit that even if sometimes the reactions from these "friends" were not what she hoped they would be, it was at least nice to have enough of a relationship with any of them for there to be an argument. That meant that she finally felt like somebody saw something of value in her besides Dad.

As the decades passed, there were questions, of course. Nobody knew how she maintained her youthful appearance—the rumors around town were that she had sold her soul to the devil. She let everybody believe what they wanted. The truth was, that little book taught her some powerful spells. An elixir of youth wasn't too complicated—if you had the recipe.

After Dad died, the bodies stopped showing up. That meant nothing but a new challenge to Carly. What it did not mean was that she should stop growing her collection. Why should she ever stop? She was doing good work in the world, even if sometimes the people she was helping didn't agree. The question became how to acquire new souls.

She started hanging out around the cemetery at the edge of town when a funeral was scheduled to take place. Sometimes, that worked. Usually, it did not. People who had someone to care for them in their death weren't as easy to re-bind as somebody without any connections meaningful enough to make them wish to stay. She thought of herself as a sort of reaper of lost souls, and why should that ever end?

Eventually, the graveyard felt unsatisfying, both because of the unpredictable number of funerals in a small town, and because even if there was a service, those were not easy spirits to bind. It was much better to find someone who was not expecting it. And that is how the shift happened. She might as well cut out the middleman and make things easier on herself. This was the ultimate public service, after all.

The first time Carly killed someone, it wasn't so much a murder as a lucky accident. Margie asked to go out and spend some time in the forest. There wasn't a reason to say no to a hike, so they went. Margie was like the mother and grandmother that she missed out on growing up. The two walked along the peaceful hiking trail, talking, and laughing. This was exactly what Carly had wished her life was like before discovering the leather book.

"Oh, look Margie! Let's go over that way. I bet we'll get a great view. We're pretty high up."

As they looked out over the valley, a man came running down the trail. He saw them standing at the overlook and must not have realized there was nothing after where they stood except vast open space. It had been a while since she'd added anybody new to her family and this seemed like it could be a good opportunity to do just that.

"Hey!" Carly called.

She waved at the man.

"Yeah, hi," he said.

He gestured that he'd like her to move off the middle of the trail and she didn't argue. That was how Kevin went home with her. He sailed off the cliff that was just beyond her and landed in a heap at the bottom of that long fall. Almost before he reached the ground, she'd pricked her finger and found just the right plant. Margie stood frozen in place, horrified at what had just happened. As soon as the man went from moaning to panic, Carly knew he'd separated from his body, and she began the incantation. *Got another one.*

Kevin joining her family made Carly realize how much more interesting it was to have a hand in things, rather than just take whoever showed up. It was then that the nature of her collection started to change. Instead of a whole lot of old ladies who only missed their weekly salon appointments and old men who wanted nothing more than another cigar and a round of golf, she started generating a more curated collection.

By the time she was an old woman herself, her house was so full of plants that it took her most of the day to keep up with the watering. Sure, she didn't always feel like doing it, but that was the cost of having such a rich and fulfilling existence with as many companions as she wanted. The question became what would happen to Carly once she'd passed away. Could she reap and bind herself? If she did, who would care for her after she no longer had a physical body? She was getting old and needed to figure out how to keep her story from ever really ending.

She tried to bind herself to a nice bonsai she'd been saving for a special occasion until her fingers looked and felt like pincushions. Obviously, she was going to have to figure out a different way to go about this.

Her mind turned to that old leather book that she'd found so many years ago. What if...? But no, it would be too hard to find the right one. How would she even do that?

Carly returned to her newspaper. She liked to read about all the things that happened in her little town. Even if she lived on the edge of importance for all those people—she was there, but not somebody anyone thought of as anything beyond a decorative fixture, really. And then she saw it and knew exactly what she needed to do.

There was an ad in the classified section that said the high school was seeking a new librarian after Mrs. Lawrence disappeared. She decided to interview, though she was older than that woman herself—she knew how old Stephanie Lawrence was when she died because Carly knew Stephanie Lawrence. That woman was one of her latest additions. It didn't really matter how old Carly was, though, because she had her ways of making sure that things went her way. An infatuation spell should do the trick. All she needed was for her interviewer to want to make her happy and give her what she was after. You couldn't call love potions and such manipulation if you weren't hurting anybody. And she wasn't. Not really.

Miss Charlotte Green started her new job as the librarian at John F. Kennedy High School that following Monday, looking every bit as young as the day she'd graduated from the place so many years ago. She took note of every student who passed through those doors and into her world of books.

So many of the young people who came into her library seemed desperate or lonely, like they didn't quite fit in.

Even the popular, pretty girls and the athletic boys with the sparkling, churlish grins appeared to feel that way sometimes. But no, none of them were just the right fit. She'd have to wait and keep waiting.

No matter, she could wait. She was feeling ready to experience life beyond the physical, but she could keep drinking the elixir of youth that the book taught her how to make until just the right person came along.

And then, one day it happened.

Melody Chapman knew very early that she was different. Her mother had died when she was born, and her father wasn't far behind. She'd always been completely and utterly alone. Nobody wanted to be around some weird girl who dressed all in black and seemed more interested in hanging out at funerals than in trying to make friends with the living. And it was true—that world certainly held more appeal for her.

The people she met after everybody had gone home at the end of the funeral were always friendly. They never seemed to notice her worn-out clothes or her bruises. It was okay that she only ever saw them the one time because maybe that's all they had to give her before they moved on. Those conversations lived in Melody's heart, and she would re-visit them again and again to remind herself that she mattered and was not just a figment of her own imagination. She also had the ability to heal things in nature. When she discovered that a hurt or wilted plant could be made whole again if she focused on it, those plants became her friends.

She spent lunch in the library—partly because she loved to read and knew that it would be nearly empty then, and partly because she didn't have anything to eat for lunch anyway, most of the time. Melody would have loved to spend hours in that library, but this would have to do.

She had heard about people learning how to control forces bigger than themselves. Sometimes, that might even involve thinning the veil between the living and the dead. On the shelf in front of her, there was a leatherbound book with symbols carved into it that she had never seen. She flipped through it and opened it to a page entitled Spirit Binding.

This book seemed much more useful than anything else she'd found at the library. Clearly, someone had left that book on the shelf to be discovered. It didn't belong there. She checked to see if anybody was looking and started to slip it into her backpack, when a handwritten note fell out. It was from Miss Green, the school librarian, and was addressed to her. It said:

Melody,

There are not many people like us in the world—those who are meant to be caretakers of what came before us, and who possess the gifts to fully embrace that role. You and I are much more alike than you might think. I have some things that would be helpful for your journey. Please come to my house after school because I would like to share them with you. It's the big, green Victorian house with the purple shutters at the top of the hill—you can't miss it.

Charlotte Green

Melody looked up at the librarian and started to ask one of the thousands of questions swirling around in her mind. Miss Green raised her eyebrows and looked at the letter in Melody's hand. The girl nearly dropped it when more words started to appear.

DO NOT come talk to me about this here or give any indication to anyone that anything unusual has happened. There will be plenty of time for answering questions later. Will you come?

Melody looked at Miss Green again and made a subtle nod, and just like that, the letter was merely a blank piece of paper in her hand. The leather book went into her backpack, and she spent the rest of the day unable to think about anything else.

Many years had passed since Melody helped Carly begin her life beyond the physical. She loved her house and all the old friends who lived there with her. She could feel that the time was short for her to find the next keeper of the book. After Melody finished making rounds with the watering can like she did every day, she settled into her ritual of afternoon tea and a crossword puzzle. She flipped through the newspaper, glancing at one story and then another. In the classified section, there was a listing looking for a new librarian over at the high school.

A Choice (The Dreamcaster)

Deborah Hetrick Catanese

The Dreamcaster got my attention then,
saying I could either watch or reenact that scene,
the one where he kissed me in the cafeteria.

"Reenact as in re-live?" I asked the wizard
who replied,
However you wish to call it, you'd feel it again.

"Yes," I said, choice made easy.
And there he was, swaggering toward me,
ignoring all the others at the homecoming dance,
the manic rhythm of Woolly Bully
sounding more like an enchanting echo on the wind
as the scene slowly blurred
as all well-spun backdrops do.
Now only his naughty movie star smile,
now his lips,
my attention seized like a bird with a broken wing
in a giant's hand,
the fleshsoft touch of his lips opening mine,
and as I realized with astonishment
that I could direct the dream by returning his passion
I kissed him for then,
I kissed him for the years apart,
I kissed with belief returned

that it could always be this kiss,
before I knew how he would fold his tent,
before my heart broke when his heart seized.
Here, now, I could stay in unconscious retreat,
and live forever in unknowing devil-may-care.

Oh, the generosity of the Dreamcaster,
allowing me to sink into such
life-loving lips,
allowing me to think for much longer than usual
that this would be the good dream
with the good heart
that keeps on beating!

THE BEDFORD CURE

Kathleen Shoop

1931

Phanie Randolph clutched the rumble seat, knuckles white. The first time out of the city, she'd been nauseated and sweating for hours. Jerking and bouncing through the Allegheny Mountains in a flimsy, though once stunning carriage brought coughing spells, motion sickness, and doubt that agreeing to this trip had been wise.

Turning onto Sweet Root Road, the sense of passing through a fairytale portal hit her. Familiar Pittsburgh smoke and smog odors were replaced with bucolic wild rose, cucumber and honeysuckle. Green hillsides walled a verdant valley. The scent of peppermint soothed. Wheels crunching over pea-gravel paths, they skirted Naugle's Mill, hugging Shober's Run and the world seemed brighter. She rubbed her eyes as Bedford Springs Resort came into view.

The buildings, trimmed with wooden railings, three stories high, awed. Queen Anne, Italianate, and Greek Revival buildings, just as Mrs. Carlson had schooled her. Hundreds of guest rooms with private baths were set within houses made of clapboard and stone and strung end to end along the great lawn.

Phanie's boss and sponsor of this trip had showed her photos from the summer the Carlsons met at the resort. The summer their lives changed forever.

Phanie dragged a handkerchief across the back of her neck. A sudden release from motion sickness allowed a moment to believe that maybe everything she'd heard was true.

"Nonsense," she said to herself as she got to her knees. She couldn't deny the grounds were beautiful. That was true. The lawn that unfolded from the resort between Constitution and Federal Hills was dotted with guests playing croquet and horseshoes. Women in summer white and sorbet-colored dresses mingled with men in seersucker suits and straw hats as they waited in line to take the Bedford Cure.

Leon, the driver, shouted over his shoulder as he pulled to a stop. "Them folks back there's lined up to take the waters at the Sulphur Spring, Miss Phanie. Will do your belly good." He slowed the horses to a stop under the portico.

"That's what they say." Phanie stretched her aching legs, then her neck, turning this way and that to find the best angle out of the wagon. She heaved one leg into position and was going to swing the other when Leon took her hand. She resisted the urge to bat him away. Like every kindhearted person—when they saw her legs were made crooked with rheumatism—they wanted to help.

She squeezed Leon's hand. "I can do it."

"It's proper to help a lady. Got nothing to do with..." he nodded toward her feet.

She glared, making him release her. "*I'm* the helper here. Mrs. Carlson didn't hire me for nothing." She knew in fact she had been hired for nothing except the smallest bit of pity, a favor to her mother who'd been in the family's employ until her death.

He lifted his hands in surrender. "Your mama would be proud of how you've taken her place. Mighty proud."

Phanie was determined to make herself as useful as she could to the widow Carlson. She splashed down onto the gravel. One foot shot out and she clung to the wagon handle, steadying herself. Leon pretended not to notice, whistling and surveying the thick forest hiding the paths that wound up Constitution Hill.

"Got a sense about things like this, Miss Phanie, and I know when I come fetch you you'll be right as rain."

She sighed, not wanting to spoil his optimism with her very practical view of how the rheumatism twisted her legs and weakened her in the most inconvenient ways. Most inconvenient was the way she continually disappointed others with her lack of health improvement.

Resort guests spied Margaret Carlson's hat long before they noticed her. Wearing a Gibson styled, feather drenched, dusty lid that was last donned when she and the mister met at the springs, her aged, spindly body seemed to struggle just to stay upright. She couldn't resist wearing the hat as she returned to Bedford for the first time in decades.

She pretended she didn't see Phanie struggling to shuffle behind lugging two carpetbags, knowing her lady's maid lived on endless springs of inner pride. Mrs. Carlson leaned on her black umbrella that she had fitted with an old boot on the end so it would stand up straight when she needed both hands. When it rained she opened the umbrella, providing enough shelter for two. "Ally oop," she greeted hotel and desk staff.

Those who remembered the odd greeting snapped around, grinning. Hugs and hand shaking stopped her every pace or so and gave Phanie a chance to move more confidently. The pauses provided Mrs. Carlson the opportunity to hide her shallow breaths.

The manager, Mr. Hancock, sauntered toward them, snapping his fingers, signaling bellhops to relieve Phanie of the luggage. She yanked back on the bag handles. Mrs. Carlson pulled Phanie's sleeve. "Fork it over, this is the best trip you'll ever have and I intend to see you enjoy every moment."

The manager shook a finger. "Ally oop to you, Mrs. Carlson. You look just as you did thirty years ago. A vision then and now."

Mrs. Carlson looked down at her outdated, long, heavy bombazine mourning dress. Like the hotel which was a bit drab with the downturn of the markets, she certainly knew her clothing had left fashion behind, but she wouldn't overspend in the Depression years and her choices had honored the love of her life. She wasn't about to have something new made so close to what she imagined was her coming dirt sleep.

"Where's that debonair husband of yours?"

Mrs. Carlson took Hancock's hands. "Swept into the afterlife on a stiff spring breeze."

He gasped.

"But just this year. The Bedford Cure healed him. Remember? For decades he was hale as northwest winds in winter."

Tears welled in Mr. Hancock's eyes. "Oh, I remember. I'm happy to hear the cure held for so long."

"With a vice grip."

He patted her.

"This trip is for my dear assistant, Phanie Randolph."

He gave Phanie a little bow.

"She needs every bit of magic the resort can stir up. Deserves it."

Phanie started to object, but Mrs. Carlson plugged her palm against Phanie's chest. "I've booked her a porch room, and with the Strawberry Moon coming in a couple weeks, with the waters, and your hospitality, she'll find peace and restoration. Beguiling. Bedford will surely wash her in beguilement."

Hancock stepped aside and cut his hand through the air to guide their way. "Our seven curing springs await."

Mrs. Carlson immediately felt at home and knew the expected enchantment would come. She had two weeks before the full moon, two weeks to gather what she needed.

Once unpacked, Phanie did as she was told and left Mrs. Carlson under the care of resort staff and fellow guests, playing cards on the porch. Her employer's *ally oops* rang out in the valley with every hand she won and "aww shucks" when she lost. The raspy voice only got lost when Phanie was led deeper into the forest to take the clear, cold limestone waters. Each medicinal spring was comprised of slightly different minerals: a little magnesium in that one, a little more sulphur in this one and pure sweetness in another.

Phanie told herself to enjoy each taste, to welcome the company of people her age. The men and women in her group were from Washington, D.C. Born to a wealthy class and untouched by the early Depression years, they continued to return each summer, staying for months. Phanie was quiet, listening to their banter and inside jokes, enjoying them even though she was on the outside. They were warm to her, stepping aside and waiting for her slowness as they crossed bridges and passed through bright-painted, Victorian-style turnstiles.

Not once did the group roll their eyes or sigh frustratingly as Phanie's bad leg dragged up mountain paths. One girl, Eugenia, and her fiancé were especially mindful, asking Phanie about how she came to come to the springs, their faces conveying concern at hearing of her mother's demise and excitement at her subsequent hiring on with Mrs. Carlson.

As the crew moved along taking waters at each spring, they simply let Phanie be in their company, making her feel comfortable and capable. It didn't take long before she was even able to swallow her embarrassment at wearing a sooty white dress that shouted her usual steel mill proximity.

None of the group seemed to care that she didn't come from the same money that they did. Whether it was dinner or afternoon tea, the fellow couples and singles welcomed her as though she too summered there yearly.

Phanie took the waters at the Sulphur, Limestone, Magnesia, Crystal, Iron, and even the Sweet Spring which was the best water she'd ever tasted. When she became too tired to make it all the way up the mountain to the Black Spring, she sat at the fork in the path and the group returned with a glass bottle of water for her to drink.

The first several mornings Phanie took to the springs with the group. Walking, even though difficult as her rheumatism made it, changed how she saw the world. The quiet woodsy moments let her mind unravel and gave her the chance to see it was none of her business that when she glimpsed Mrs. Carlson's ledger she saw that this trip would exhaust the last of the woman's Mellon Bank account.

It was none of Phanie's business when the Carlson children phoned saying that this three-week stay was ridiculous and that their mother should go to North Carolina with them instead of galivanting around the Pennsylvania countryside with the "help."

When Phanie agreed with their arguments Mrs. Carlson snapped, "Keep your nose out of my concerns. It's my retreat, my money, my life. I choose you."

The woman snatched up the phone, barked orders to the operator to connect her back to her daughter and shouted into the receiver, "Phanie Randolf deserves this trip. She and her mother before her have been here, kind, and loving to your father and me. They've been *here*. End of discussion."

Mrs. Carlson slammed down the phone and then bolted from the parlor, the umbrella cane with the boot clomping over the hardwoods like a third foot. She only paused her storming exit when the coughing took hold yet again.

Phanie was so grateful for the trip even though she didn't believe in the healing powers of simple water, no matter where it sprang from or what minerals it comprised. She didn't believe the story of how Mr. Carlson was instantly cured of his blood disease and feebleness by drinking and bathing in the springs. But she loved that the Carlsons had met there and that Mr. Carlson's health improved in a seemingly otherworldly way. Phanie attributed his turnaround to incredible healing luck or magical leeches or simple, powerful love that had made and kept him well until old age.

Phanie was taking another round of water from the Magnesia Spring when she decided to try harder to believe in the cure. Mrs. Carlson and every single person who she met at the Springs had faith that the waters might ease Phanie's rheumatism, somehow straighten her joints. So, after a week, Phanie decided she would embrace the possibility.

Though exhilarated, the amount of time it took to move to each spring still exhausted her. Seven days into taking the cure, she snaked along the paths, determined to make it to the Black Spring. But when her leg gave out, she managed to catch herself on the tree trunk and again, sat, dejected at her rebelling body.

When Eugenia saw that Phanie had stopped, she mopped Phanie's brow with a crisp hankie. "We'll get the water for you and one of these mornings you'll do it." Eugenia, Tom, and the other group-mates bounded away and returned with a bottle for Phanie.

As she drank it down, Eugenia and Tom took the opportunity to stand so close to each other that Phanie could see the love blooming inside their whispered words, their clasped fingers, and their private giggles as they swam in the freedom that retreating at the Bedford Springs brought.

Once the group returned to the hotel, they moved on to the next activity—cards and lemonade on the porch or a trip to town on the Talley-Ho.

For the seventh day, hotel staff encouraged Phanie to stay with the gang but she settled on a chaise lounge with lemonade and *Pride and Prejudice* instead. She'd barely read a word before she exhaled and submerged into sleep.

Next thing she knew, someone was shaking her awake, pawing at the hem of her dress. She pushed to sitting, wiping drool from her cheek. A little girl with a jump rope took Phanie's book and ran. Her little laugh rang out, the glorious sound captured between the hillsides. She looked back as she ran. "Come play!"

Phanie yelled for the girl to return the book and then clamped a hand over her mouth, embarrassed for screaming out. Before she could stop herself she was rushing after the girl, dragging her leg along, feeling the aches that came from long walks through the woods. She caught up with the girl behind some boxwoods where chairs had been arranged for more private seating. The sprite was there pumping water from what must have been another spring, one that hadn't been on Phanie's list to take.

She giggled. "I'm Anna. Pump so I can drink."

Phanie grumbled but did it. She quickly regretted being nice because Anna cupped water and tossed it onto Phanie. The coldness sent a chill through her and she reached for Anna who disappeared through the boxwoods again. At least she'd left the book behind. Phanie snatched it up and limped toward the porch.

Back at her chaise, the manager's assistant, Jack Lambert, scuttled over with a towel. He snatched the jump rope off the ground. "You're feeling very well after taking the waters, aren't you?"

She gestured. "Oh, no. That's not mine. A little girl. It's hers. She took the book. *Pride and Prejudice* I was reading it and... well, I chased her to that spring by the boxwood and..."

"By the—?"

"Not one of them on the map, but..."

He waved to couples headed toward the indoor swimming pool. "There's no spring there."

She rubbed her temples feeling foolish. "But—"

Had she dreamt it?

"Girl's name is Anna." She looked down to see her white dress splattered with water. Confused, she surveyed the area where she'd been reading and napping and laughed. "I swear I got the book back from her and..."

He dropped to one knee and groped under the chaise. When he straightened and his eyes met hers, the intensity made her stomach flip-flop.

He looked at her lips. "You are so beautiful."

Stunned to be told such a thing by a man so close she could smell his spicy soap, Phanie had no response. She clasped a hand over her chest to keep her heart from thumping out of her body.

"The springs agree with you very much," he said, shyly looking away.

"Thank you."

He snapped to standing. "I'll keep an eye out for your book. But the reason I came to you was to let you know that Mrs. Carlson had an early meal and went to bed. She ordered sandwiches for you to have on the porch outside your room."

He offered his arm to escort Phanie, but she just shook her head, wondering if he'd actually said she was beautiful. Had she lost her mind? The day's heat and the walk had clearly been too much.

Phanie ate cucumber sandwiches and gazpacho for dinner. The shared porch connected her room to other guest rooms in Anderson House, stretching down the entire length of the building. Unnerved by the strange dream she'd had about the girl, she relaxed in the rocking chair and added honey to her chamomile tea. She rubbed her legs with the lotion that Jack had delivered as she was finishing her meal.

Laughter and voices on the great lawn curled up to her porch. People gathered round a firepit and walked along the pea gravel paths as it gently began to rain. The scent of it stirred Phanie, making her grateful that she'd been invited on such a decadent trip. She'd never be able to repay Mrs. Carlson in any way other than being the best assistant that she could.

Phanie acknowledged she felt more relaxed than she could remember. She didn't even feel left out of the groups and couples and laughing singles playing late night card games down below. Her world had expanded since she'd arrived at the Springs. The whole place seemed to breathe and stand alive in the fresh air like no other setting in her life. And though no closer to a cure, it simply didn't matter.

In bed that night, Phanie turned to her side, a sliver of space between the damask drapes inviting moonlight to fall over the bed. Something about that seventh night lent a sense of peace, a goodness she hadn't felt since her mother died.

Two nights before the full moon, Margaret Carlson snuck out just before midnight. Wrapped in a thick terry cloth robe supplied by the resort, thumping along with her booted cane, she took the porch to where it wrapped around the end of Anderson House.

Her tiny lantern barely lit her boots but with the nearly full moon it was enough. She crept down the stairs and shuffled toward the Sulphur Spring. She felt every year of her age and the weak lungs screamed with every shaky footfall, but she was thrilled at what she was about to do. She edged her way behind the spring house, the umbrella cane providing just enough support to navigate the uneven ground.

She paused. A soft breeze tickled the back of her neck, giving the sensation that used to come when Edgar brushed his lips over her skin. She whipped around nearly losing her balance. "Edgar?"

He was not there, but his spirit was and she knew she was doing the right thing. Each carefully placed step invited her deeper into memories of her husband, the way he'd loved her from that first time in the Black Spring and then for the rest of his life.

The ground grew wetter. Mrs. Carlson huffed and puffed, her foot slipping on stones as she got closer to the spring. She lifted the lantern to better illuminate the stone outcropping. She panicked, not seeing the mark. Had she gone to the wrong side? Closer. She squinted. Closer.

There.

She giggled. The hearts. She and Edgar had etched them into the stone with their initials swirled together at the center. She traced the grooves of the letters, a closeness to her absent husband filling her. As she sighed, relieved to have found it, the lantern went dark. She looked skyward. The nearly full moon was bright enough. She got to her hands and knees. The scent of mud filled her nose.

"Oh, Edgar, look at me now."

Below the hearts she tossed pebbles and clay away from the wall, revealing a hollow. Her laughter stirred the young woman inside her and she dug like a dog. Mushroom and rich soil flew, the earthy scent drawing her back thirty years.

She'd widened the gap between stone and ground further, got to her belly, and reached inside. The insides of the hill smelled stronger of moss and worms and she thought for sure she was about to get a nip on her fingertips from a chipmunk or snake. Common sense would have told her to stop this nonsense, but sense had nothing to do with it.

"I've come this far, Edgar." She fumbled for the bundle, fingers bounding back and forth, stretching. Was it even still there?

She heaved forward and finally felt the canvas, moist, but present. She wrenched it out and got to her knees, moon rays brightening the treasure.

Musty, moldy fabric released its fragrance as she unwrapped it. A book and a glass bottle.

"Ally oop."

She hugged the items and looked over her shoulder. She would have sworn on Bibles in court that Edgar was right there with there.

"My miracle."

Phanie woke before dawn and pulled a quilt around her shoulders, the lavender laundry soap they used at the hotel embedding in her mind. Heading toward the door that led to the porch she tripped over the rug, her bad leg betraying her just as it always did. She stared at the rug. "Blame it." She had rolled it up after the first day she tripped over it, but housekeeping must have rolled it back into place sometime the previous day when Phanie was out of the room.

The screen door squeaked open and she stepped into the cool morning air. She was startled to find Mrs. Carlson sitting on the porch rocking, sipping lemon and peppermint tea, the blue hotel robe pulled tight to her neck.

"How lovely," Mrs. Carlson said. "I *thought* you might waken early too. Tell me how you're faring."

Phanie hadn't found a cure, but she had found unexpected wonderment on the serene forest paths and glee at making new friends. "I feel alive here, like you said I would. I can breathe."

Mrs. Carlson eyed Phanie's feet.

She wanted to report something better. "No. Nothing's really changed with my legs. Just feel better in spite of it. And I'm so grateful that you brought me."

"Trip isn't over yet." Mrs. Carlson patted the rocking chair beside her. "We'll have tea and watch the sun rise."

Phanie added honey to her teacup and noticed a satchel at Mrs. Carlson's feet and that she was wearing mud-caked boots. "What on earth?"

"Yes, yes, I went for a little midnight walk. Don't tattle on me. I'm sane as you."

Phanie choked on a sip of tea. "You could have been hurt."

Mrs. Carlson gestured to her umbrella cane standing up near the railing. "Trusty umbrella did me right."

"Your children will skewer me if—"

"Shush. Let's not talk about them."

Mrs. Carlson poured more tea for Phanie and opened the satchel. She pulled out a bottle with a torn label. Phanie shifted the lantern on the table closer and recognized the trademark—a lion and a unicorn on their hindlegs with the words Che Sara Sara linking them along the bottom of the logo. Mrs. Carlson poured water into a large glass insisting Phanie drink three.

"Don't you want some?"

She shook her head, a slow smile reaching her lips. "Oh, sweet Phanie. I had my share."

Phanie shrugged and finished the third glass. "What's that?"

"My book. Rescued it and this water from behind the Sulphur Spring. Just where Edgar and I buried it thirty years ago."

Phanie lifted her glass. "This water is thirty years old?"

"Best I ever had. Just like the day we bottled it at..."

Phanie finished her sentence. "The Black Spring. The gang brings me some every day and I'd recognize its taste anywhere."

Phanie had amazed herself. "And your book?" She reached for the satchel.

Mrs. Carlson stepped on it. "Later. For now, take your cure and rest your bones. Once you've had your full-moon bath we will share the book."

On the night of the full moon Phanie readied just as Mrs. Carlson ordered. She layered her lightest weight chemise and dress and waited at the base of the stairs that led to the Magnesia Spring. Phanie was shocked when Mrs. Carlson didn't bring Hancock or a butler or Jack Lambert to take them in a mule-drawn wagon up the mountain to the Black Spring.

Instead, the old woman plugged her umbrella cane on the first stair and headed upward. She turned. Her old-fashioned blue hat was crinkled and smelled of mothballs. Phanie recognized it as the one Mr. Carlson had bought her here at the springs when they met. This blue hat and the resort robe provided the only color she'd worn since her husband passed.

"Waiting for an engraved invite, are you?"

Phanie chuckled and followed the woman, the two of them keeping similar pace. Phanie held the lantern as they serpentined up Constitution Hill. Mrs. Carlson lifted her cane when they reached the fork in the path that Phanie had yet to take.

Mrs. Carlson tapped Phanie's bottom with the umbrella. "Soon you'll feel well enough to go to the Black Spring and the overlook with the others."

Phanie pulled deep breaths, barely able to concede she heard the statement. Her legs groaned and lungs burned, the humid air feeling as though it was baking her from the inside out. Crickets and tree frogs sounded in the woods as the blend of peppermint, honeysuckle, hyacinth and cucumber intoxicated her. "I can do it."

They turned down a path that jutted off from the main one. "This way." Mrs. Carlson looked at her pocket watch. "Three hours down and we'll make it to the Black Spring just in time for the fullest moon imaginable. It doubles and triples the effects of the water. You'll see."

If Phanie had had the energy she would have argued that it was pure slag that the water or the moon could do any such thing. Yes, the clean forest air and heady scents of woodland summer, the lemonade and naps and cheerful company had lightened her mood and given her new perspective, but to consider that she might be healed of a ten-year affliction that twisted her leg and kept her tripping over even a thin summer rug, was a waste of time.

Mrs. Carlson slowed her pace then stopped, leaning on the umbrella. "Ally oop."

Phanie followed the older woman's gaze. Moonbeams rained down on a raised stone bed. The stillness in the deep, full-moonlit morning revealed water pouring. She could see the surface of the bed was actually water.

"Black Spring," Phanie whispered, stunned by its beauty.

"Spills 600,000 gallons of water a day." Mrs. Carlson pointed her cane. "Hancock told me they were going to divert it to make a lake and continue to water the golf course with it. So I knew we had to climb up here to get the best of it. And look." She raised her arms. "Perfect moon, just for you."

Phanie felt as though the heavens were lifting her off her feet. Upturned face, she was overwhelmed. Tears fell down her cheeks. Moved. There was no other way to describe how she felt other than to say something inside her shifted and tingled and thrilled her.

Mrs. Carlson dug a hankie from her cuff and dabbed at Phanie's face. "Listen up. You've the most wonderful life in front of you. Just take the waters, bask in the moonglow and you'll see."

"But..."

"No buts."

The two staggered toward the spring—one hampered by age and the other by illness. Mrs. Carlson began removing her clothes and instead of protesting, Phanie did the same. Down to their skins they slipped into the rectangle water bed and floated. Light winds pulled thin cottony clouds past the magnificent moon, weaving between oak and sugar maple tree tops, the stars peeking through.

"Magic," Phanie said as her skin tickled with hope and excitement at the heavenly bodies and forest scents. She wiggled her toes and turned her ankles and wrists, the buoyancy relieving pain and stiffness.

With the Black Spring waters spilling into the pool, Phanie sculled to stay afloat. The women talked and Mrs. Carlson revealed the way she and her husband first felt love for one another. Turns out a rivalry gave way to affection as they'd fought over who got to use the springs first on that full moon night thirty years before. Phanie wheezed with laughter.

"Oh yes, right from the start both of us were stubborn mules. Should have seen us. Gratefully no one did, because we had ripped off our clothes and leapt right in, utterly inappropriate, but we wanted the cure. We wanted each other."

Mrs. Carlson's words trailed off before she began again. "The moon-splashed cure was given to us by an older woman we'd played cards with earlier that week. She'd gifted us that very book I mentioned the other day. The moon water cure demanded we bathe under its full glow while in the Black Spring."

Mrs. Carlson's voice softened. "We kept a decent distance, don't get me wrong. But it was beautiful." She held her hand into the moonlight. Water droplets trailed off the ends of her fingers. She almost looked as though someone was reaching back toward her. "Just our fingertips touching and caressing as we told our life stories and fell in love. Right here."

Phanie was honored to be trusted with this story.

"Edgar's illness dissipated. Instantly. It's mad, I know, but it did. That very night, God shook the earth, changing its axis for the two of us. Dramatic but true. And as directed in the book, when the sun was just an hour from rising, we filled a bottle where the spring gushes into the pool right there. We headed back down the mountain and added our story to the book before wrapping it in the canvas and tucking it into the hollow in the outcropping. We marked the stones with two hearts joined with our initials."

Phanie exhaled, feeling something hopeful emerging, something joyful. This time Phanie believed the story about the Carlsons. It *had* to be true. Hearing the tale in this way, in this place, she now believed Edgar had been cured by the waters.

Mrs. Carlson ran her fingers over the surface of the spring. "You aren't the only skeptic. His doctors back in Pittsburgh were in disbelief. They hadn't thought he'd live to be thirty." She went on with the parts of their story that

Phanie already knew, the woman's voice and familiar words lulling Phanie into floating sleep.

Phanie wakened slowly, still hovering on the water's surface, aware and not aware of exactly where she was. Magic. She remembered what Mrs. Carlson had divulged. She'd felt the power of the moon bath, the chilly water lapping against her skin. The magnificent sky still flush with stars and moon glow and she admitted to it right then.

She believed. She lifted her arms skyward. "Ally oop."

When she didn't hear Mrs. Carlson return the greeting, Phanie looked to her side. Mrs. Carlson was gone.

Jack Lambert appeared through the trees, carrying a towel. He held it up so she would have privacy. "I won't look. Promise."

Phanie was mortified and worried, but she climbed over the stones onto the grass, arms across her chest. Dressing quickly, she nearly ripped her chemise. "Did you already put Mrs. Carlson in the cart? She's already dressed? I'm so embarrassed and I can't believe I... you didn't see me like... this?"

"No, what? I mean, yes, I'm doing as Mrs. Carlson instructed, yes. I'm following my orders."

Phanie yanked her linen dress over wet skin thinking that sounded right—Mrs. Carlson barking orders.

"She fetched me and said to come up here to get you. That you'd taken the moon bath in the Black Spring and—"

"Mrs. Carlson walked to the bottom?" Impossible. "While I slept?" Phanie searched the sky for the moon's movements, seeing that it was getting low, but couldn't believe she would have slept that long. "I don't understand."

Jack offered his arm. She took it, wanting to move quickly. He helped her into the front seat of the wagon and ran his hand through his hair. Tendrils sprang this way and that, clearly having hopped out of bed and drove up the mountain in a rush.

He shook the reins to get the mules moving. "I woke up to her knocking. She was standing at my door with that blue hat, a bag and her cane, giving me orders to head up here. I did as I was told. You better believe."

Phanie chuckled and yawned. What a night it had been. "But..."

She was too confused to shape her thoughts into coherent words so she kept quiet. She would get the story from Mrs. Carlson in the morning over tea, she was sure. She rubbed her ankle where it made its crooked turn. Perhaps the cure only worked for the Carlsons.

Jack helped Phanie into Anderson House. She did her best to force her bad leg to cooperate. No pain, but the dragging remained. But pain-free was *something*. They passed Mrs. Carlson's door and the umbrella cane stood outside it with the satchel.

He scooped them up and when Phanie entered her room, he set the items inside. "Don't want those to go missing."

Phanie eyed the bag. "Surely not." She was suddenly embarrassed at how he'd found her at the spring.

As if he read her mind he raised his hand. "Didn't see a thing, I swear. But I'm so glad it was you who got to take the strawberry moon bath in Black Spring this year."

"This year? You know about the... others?"

He nodded. "Bedford Springs has its share of secrets." He paused. "They're revealed to those who need them most."

His gaze made her cheeks go warm as she remembered him telling her she was beautiful the day she'd met the girl, Anna.

"Very glad it was you," he said and closed the door.

She put her palm against the wood door, wishing he was still in the room. "And I'm very glad it was you, Jack."

Phanie wakened to pounding on the door. Sunlight outlined the drapes. "Blame it." She'd slept too long. The knocking continued. Mrs. Carlson must have been angry at her leisureliness after such a magical night.

Or was her boss in need? Phanie threw back the blankets and hopped out of bed. She'd gripped the doorknob before she realized she hadn't tripped. Had she rolled up the rug before she went to sleep? She looked over her shoulder.

The rug was down.

And she hadn't tripped.

She looked at her feet, shaking her bad leg. Still crooked, but without its numbing pain she put weight on it then rocked back and leaned on it again. No pain.

And she hadn't tripped.

The knocking came again, harder. "Miss Randolf? Phanie? Please answer."

She smoothed her hair and opened the door. Hancock was there, fists balled at his sides. "I have to—"

She pointed toward the rug near the bed. "I didn't trip. This morning... the rug and—"

"Miss Phanie. Please, I don't know what to say... but Mrs. Carlson."

Phanie craned to see past him. Was Mrs. Carlson so angry that she'd sent someone to fetch her?

He took her by the shoulders. "She passed last night."

"She..."

"I'm so sorry."

The realization settled in. "You mean Mrs. Carlson?"

Tears shone in his eyes.

"Died, passed like that, you mean?"

He yanked Phanie into a hug, squeezing the breath right out of her.

The events of the night before flashed through her mind.

They let go of each other and she glanced at the umbrella cane standing to the side, the satchel beside it.

"Are you sure?"

"Quite."

Mrs. Carlson had been bursting with energy the night before. "But how? I don't..."

"We know she was out of her room at some point. People saw you two at the bridge leading to Magnesia Spring. After that... it wasn't until."

"Jack..."

"He told me she came to his room. Ordered him to fetch you..." Hancock looked at Phanie's feet, then past her to the rug. His eyes widened. "And you didn't trip. It worked? It worked. The full moon and..."

Phanie couldn't stop herself from crying. Devastated by Mrs. Carlson's death, grateful for the gift she'd been given. She couldn't piece together what had happened, how it happened. How had Mrs. Carlson traversed the mountain so quickly after bathing in the spring?

Dizzied, Phanie grabbed for the door to steady herself. "Can I talk to Jack? Please?"

Hancock snapped his heels together as though the movement brought him back to himself, regrouping into the man she'd known since arriving at Bedford. "At once."

Jack and Phanie had lunch on the porch outside the colonnade and recounted what both experienced the night before.

Jack sipped tea. "I know for sure the Mrs. Carlson who came to my door last night was flesh and bone." He took a bite of carrot cake. "I mean, I think... she had to have been... right? The dust was still shaking off those million feathers on that hat of hers. Gruff voice. No one else wears something like that around here. I was pretty tired, but it was her."

Phanie drank her magnesia water, but only pushed food around her plate. "And I know for sure she led me to the Black Spring."

"So then..."

They stared at each other for some time.

"I guess we'll never know." Phanie's mind went to the fact she no longer had a job. She put her palm to the nape of her neck, afraid she might burst into tears.

Jack reached into his pocket and took out a deck of cards. "Today's my day off. Will you play? One hand to take your mind off of what comes next."

Phanie exhaled deeply. Mrs. Carlson's children. "Her family will have a fit."

The snap of Jack's expert shuffling mixed with the birdsong.

"They didn't want Mrs. Carlson coming here with me. She spent every last dime on this trip. Emptied her bank account right out."

Jack dealt the cards. "You gave her absolute joy. She wanted this—healing for you, memories for her. You'll add to the book—there's still time before the full moon is completely gone. I'll help you bury it and the bottle filled with last night's water and..." He shrugged.

"You filled a bottle for me?"

"Went right back up the hill after I dropped you at your room."

No one besides Mrs. Carlson had ever done such a thing for her. Mrs. Carlson and Jack. Two treasures she couldn't have fathomed just months before.

"You'll stay here."

Phanie refolded her napkin into a tiny square. "Here?"

"I mean, if you want. I mean going forward. Not just right this minute. There's plenty of work here even with the world crumbling in on itself."

She looked into the distance. Cardinals and blue jays swooped and looped over the great lawn. Crows chased them, squawking. The humid air carried the scent of cucumber mint and honeysuckle. Hilarity rang out down the porch closer to the golf course. Eugenia and Tom waved as they headed for the rope swing hanging from an oak across from the Limestone Spring.

Jack dealt a final card and studied her. "Tell me this doesn't feel like home."

She twirled her bad ankle, feeling flexibility she couldn't remember ever having even as a child.

She couldn't deny it. "It does." She smiled at Jack, the way he regarded her every bit as intoxicating as the moon bath and Black Spring waters. "It feels exactly like home."

With Leon driving them, Phanie and Jack attended Mrs. Carlson's funeral in Pittsburgh. Then by autumn, the two got married beside the roaring, clear Iron Spring, making it forever known as the Wedding Grotto, shared by brides and grooms for decades forward.

Mr. and Mrs. Lambert tended to a seventy-year marriage working at Bedford Springs until it closed in 1986. Well beyond their working days, they crept to the stone outcropping behind the Sulphur Spring where they'd etched two moons joined by their initials marking where they'd buried the satchel.

Into the woods they'd go, taking full moon baths in the Black Spring until they were too old to climb the mountain, too tired to do anything except bask in the glow of each other. They lived just long enough to know that the hotel was going to reopen. And in their final days, they shared the book, the bottle, and the cure with a young couple who needed a reason to believe.

Bits of Fact and Fiction

To this very day hotel guests report seeing a woman wearing a blue hat that was fashionable over a century before. Female guests sometimes experience a tugging on their skirt or pants hems in the areas near the pool or first floor bathrooms. A little girl named Anna still lures people to play. Some find *Pride and Prejudice* in the library or in their guestroom or sitting on the table near the lobby fireplace, the book finding its way into the hands of whomever needs a little moment with a romantic read.

And when the hotel owners restored Bedford Springs (it reopened in 2007) an eighth spring was discovered—the Eternal Spring—located just below the front desk in the world-famous Springs Eternal Spa. Perhaps Anna knew something the rest of them didn't. Phanie, for one, became a believer.

LAST SEEN IN PARADISE

Cindy Hill

Warmth crept into the aircraft's cabin as the airline steward pushed open the heavy door.

"Welcome to Belize!" another flight attendant said, reminding everyone to gather their belongings and keep their passport and immigration paperwork together as they exited the aircraft.

Jules studied the photo on her phone.

"Is that her? The driver who will take us to the jungle resort?" Jules's fellow traveler, Selvy, asked as she peeked at the phone.

"Yup, that's Elba, my childhood friend," Jules replied. "She inherited the resort from her dad after he passed away a few years ago."

"If she's anything like you, I can only imagine the mischievous escapades that await us," Selvy said, pulling her backpack from the overhead compartment.

"We were always getting into trouble with my Grandma G. Mom shipped me and my sister to Grandma's every summer, and it was one of the best experiences of my life." Jules's lips curled in a smile.

"Lucky kiddos. I bet most Carolinians never heard of your mother's homeland in those days." Selvy yelped as Jules's elbow connected with her arm.

"Watch it. I'm only in my fifties, not over the century mark yet."

Jules adjusted her sunglasses as she descended the boarding stairs and stepped onto the tarmac.

"Now you get to write about those experiences and add the escapades, too," Selvy said, pushing the large brimmed hat onto her head as the warm summer sun shone more brilliantly than she had imagined.

Jules beckoned to some passengers behind her, "Follow me to immigration. I'll get us all through a little faster." She grinned. "Dual citizenship has its benefits."

Airport employees were readily available and ushered arriving passengers through lines to clear Customs.

The immigration officer arched her eyebrows, and a smile lit her face. "Jules, it's good to see you again, and this time with new friends."

"Molina, let's grab that drink before I leave," Jules said, then added to the group, "Another of my partners in crime."

"Those were the days," Molina replied, her face beaming with a smile.

After the friendly greetings, Jules pointed to the luggage area. "Let's make this fast. I hope you brought your appetite because fish panades, plantain chips and a cold beer are waiting for us down the road."

"Hey! Where's the old jalopy?" Jules flung her arms around Elba.

Two local guys were busy loading the luggage in a bus with the logo *AZUL JUNGLE RESORT*.

"Oh, it's around the corner. I'm not getting rid of that old truck anytime soon, *gal*," Elba replied.

"I brought you some company for a week." Jules made introductions of the group of writers.

Elba greeted everyone with a warm welcome.

"Can't hardly wait to trek through the jungle, and I think Jules mentioned food, beer, and other local libations," Kenny said, his thumb tipped to his lips in a drinking motion.

"Yeah, some of us are here to write, some to explore, some just to eat authentic Belize cuisine, and Kenny may indulge a bit in the latter that he mentioned," Cassie said as she sank onto the front seat.

The group erupted in laughter and piled into the bus while teasing Kenny.

"Long Boy, Charlie!" Elba called to the two men as they finished loading the last luggage.

"We have a beautiful day for traveling to the South of Belize." Elba briefed the crowd on what to expect. "About a three-hour trip ahead of us. We'll bypass the capital city of Belmopan and continue to the resort. I have a couple of stops planned along the way that I think you will enjoy, and a chance to stretch your legs. These guys will introduce themselves while I get you folks some water."

Elba opened a cooler packed with cold bottled water.

"Hey," Long Boy greeted the group. "My real name is Martin, but only Ma called me that and only when I was in bad trouble. My friends call me Long Boy because, as you can see, I'm tall." Perspiration gathered on his skin as the early afternoon humidity intensified.

"Long Boy is the bus driver, mechanic, and gardener," Elba said. "Charlie is my lead handyman, bartender, and tour guide. We all double up on duties during the off-season with smaller groups. November to May is the hectic tourist time. You've just hit our off-season. We all want you guys to relax and have fun!"

"Hello, to clarify things, I don't do all the tasks at once, but I do know how to make friends quickly," Charlie said as he opened another cooler containing two pitchers. "In addition to water, I have the fun drinks—rum punch with rum..." he lifted the first pitcher, "and this one without."

The group cheered and toasted one another, selfies and silly faces grinning back at them on their phone screens.

"I'm liking this choice of retreat already! Cheers to a week of writing in paradise. Thanks for the invite, Jules." Kenny tipped his glass of rum punch toward Jules.

She made a theatrical bow at the waist, sweeping her arms. "Thank you very much. I'm thrilled you all could make it, and I hope you accomplish some of what you have planned on your writing journey. Elba, thanks again, my friend." Jules paused for a moment. "Here, let me try speaking some Creole." Jules cleared her throat then spoke in broken English. "*We di have fun yet, or what? Mek a talk mo till you anda stan mi.*"

Jules looked around the bus as the group rushed to interpret what she said.

"Close," she replied to their guesses. "You'll hear quite a bit of Creole, and if spoken slowly, it's somewhat easy to understand."

"What did you really say?" Cassie asked.

"I asked, *Are we having fun yet, or what? Let me talk more until you understand me.*"

"Heck, I got most of that!" Kenny said with confidence.

His comment was met with teasing, and someone from the back of the bus challenged him to repeat the sentence.

"Okay, I'm not ready to be tested, but give me a week, and you'll see," he replied.

"Although we talk with an accent, everyone in Belize also speaks English, and most speak Spanish. We get visitors from all over the world, and somehow, even if they speak some other foreign language, everyone always seems to have a good time." Elba handed out bottled water. "Stay hydrated."

"Okay, folks," Charlie addressed the group. "Long Boy will do the driving, and I will give you some details about the resort and sights we pass along the way. I won't *blab* the whole way there though. If you have any questions, don't hesitate to ask."

"*Blab* means talk," Jules chimed in.

"You still remember the native tongue then," Charlie said.

"Yup! Sometimes, I use some words, and my friends crack up. Then they try to say the phrase, or a sentence and I crack up." Jules chuckled.

"On that note, I'm going to steal Jules. I know she is just dying for a ride in the jalopy. We will see how much of a local she still is since the truck has no A/C and it's almost 100 degrees today!" Elba handed Jules two bottles of water.

"Whoa, I signed up for A/C," Jules protested playfully.

"*Gal, watch ya!* A/C is only for the bus and at the resort," Elba teased.

"Aha, I know *gal* means girl—maybe *watch ya* means to look at you?" Kenny asked.

"You're learning fast," Jules replied. "But it's more like *listen,* or *be for real,* even, *hey.* Something like that."

"We're pulling out, folks. The lunch stop is about thirty minutes down the road," Charlie announced as Jules and Elba exited the bus.

"I'm ready for Belize's number one beer." Kenny pointed to the billboard. "Says it right there."

"You better Belize it! *Belikin* is the only domestic beer produced here." Charlie slipped into the role of tour guide. Next he pointed at the vast, imposing river that flowed under a bridge. "Folks, that is the Belize River. Those huge creatures in the water are manatees, known here as Sea Cows." He motioned to Long Boy to slow down, giving the group time to observe the animals bobbing in the water.

"To the left is the Caribbean. The manatees migrate into the Belize River, and as you can see, this river empties into the sea, making it possible for them to swim up the river."

"We'll grab a quick lunch at Sparky's Place, then get this show on the road," he continued.

Edna pulled in front of the resort bus and led the way onto the two-lane highway.

"Holy cow! It's hot," Jules said. She leaned out the passenger window and stretched her arm as far as she could to get some air to circulate in the truck cab.

"Summer in the tropics," Edna sighed.

"The photos you sent of the resort are beautiful!" Jules said.

"I did more than I thought, but so much needed to be done—it was necessary. I added a few new cabanas. One can be used for a relaxed vibe, yoga, or even a workspace if someone needs to work on vacation. A gym! I'm super proud of that. We renovated the swimming pool, all the rooms, and the entry." Elba maneuvered the truck around a roundabout.

"Busy," Jules replied.

"Chef needed more fresh produce, so I expanded the herb and vegetable garden and a greenhouse. It's been a challenge. Financially, it is stressful. Physically, I am exhausted. Mentally exhausted, too. I'm a pro at burning the candle at both ends, but I couldn't just have the place continue to deteriorate. It has been there over half a century. I need to keep it going. My family depends on this resort to make a living. The twins are in college now. Mom and Aunt Louisa live in the village, and I help with them. Many others need the job." A worried expression crossed Elba's face.

"You got this," Jules encouraged her friend. "You know what you are doing. Your dad taught you well, and you are smart. All the things you've worked on to improve the place—that is smart."

"More needs to be done, but it must wait until next year. I am hoping to have a good and steady summer season," Elba replied, then continued, "I miss my Juan, taken in that accident too soon. I can't believe it has been almost ten years."

"I imagine you do miss him every day," Jules responded kindly.

A few moments passed in comfortable silence.

"I can think of a few ideas for advertising if you'd like," Jules said.

"Of course! Your background is marketing, duh. Thanks, my friend."

Later, at the resort, Jules stood on the stairs near her friends. "Hello again. Let's plan to meet in the dining room in an hour. Feel free to explore the resort and pool area, or rest—whatever you'd like to do until then."

Elba caught up to Jules at the top of the stairs.

"*AZUL JUNGLE RESORT* is transformed." Jules looked around at the open space.

The lobby, with its high ceiling and exposed mahogany beams, overstuffed cushioned sofas and chairs, paintings depicting Mayan temples, coral reefs, various tropical birds and plants, and floor-to-ceiling glass windows, created an inviting space.

"Thank you so much!" Elba looked around, proudly pointing out other details in the lobby, including the stairs they stood on.

"You're writing again. I enjoy your work, and you're very good at storytelling." Elba walked alongside Jules.

"Maybe the novel I am working on will make it to the bestsellers list and the movies, then I will join you in this paradise."

"What are you working on?"

"Two women who are best friends. One is the owner of a resort in the jungle..." Jules paused as Elba interrupted her.

"Okay, fair enough. I'll wait for the book to be released."

"I can't share until then anyway. It's bad luck!" Jules exaggerated her response. "Also, I have too many ideas about the characters and what they need to do—I need to give them space and tackle the novel again tomorrow. I write best in the mornings. I'm brain-dead right now."

"It's so cool to listen to you talk about writing, and characters and building your story. Yeah, that's nuts.

Writers can create an entire universe and different worlds. It's amazing."

"I tend to stick to life lessons, and romantic comedies with some suspense, poems—that seems to be my wheelhouse." Jules unlocked her room door.

"I'll see you later, Julie Bird," Elba said, reminding Jules of the nickname they'd created when they'd first met.

"Okay, Elba Coconut," she laughed.

Later, the group gathered around communal tables, chatting and sipping tropical cocktails.

"This is an elevated pina colada. It will fit nicely with my sweet romance story," Selvy said, twirling the straw around the glass.

"What if our characters are based on our cocktails?" Cassie asked.

"Mine would be burning hot with this habanero margarita!" Jules laughed.

"Kenny's would be running for cover with his hurricane rum punch!" someone yelled from the other table.

"Got that right!" Kenny took a long sip of his drink.

"What about you, Sam?" Jules asked another writer from the group.

"I'm a beer guy. I stick to nonfiction. I'm doing something interesting mid-week. A couple of us will trek into the jungle with a tour guide, hoping to see a jaguar."

"Oh, hell no!" Cassie said, "I'll just watch Mufasa on TV."

"Hate to break it to you, Cas," Sam said. "But Mufasa is a lion in a movie. We're trekking for tigers here."

"Same answer from me." Cassie shuddered. "I can't imagine intentionally searching for a predator in its natural habitat."

"Can't say that you're wrong," Sam agreed, "I survived Mount Kilimanjaro and have been on a couple African safaris—sort of an adrenalin junkie. I've been saving this adventure for a while, and it tied nicely in with the writing retreat."

"I'm sticking with water," another from the group answered. "Bad things happen when I mix tequila with my characters."

The comment sparked loud chatter among the group, which led to new drink requests.

"Dinner!" Kenny applauded the chef.

"Fresh red snapper from the Caribbean Sea served three ways... grilled, baked, or fried." Maria led the way with staff from the kitchen.

"You'll want to save room for dessert," Elba advised as she helped distribute the various side dishes. "Maria is also a fantastic pastry chef."

"Belizeans love key lime pie. I think you will, too. I also made a pineapple upside-down cake!" She beamed as the group clapped appreciatively.

"Oh, sweet lord!" Cassie said. "I need to do some serious walking tomorrow, but it's rather warm outside."

"That won't be a problem," Elba said. "I just put in a new gym beside the pool."

Elba looked across at Jules who did a quick little clap above her head, and mouthed silently, *"You got this!"*

"I'll burn my calories off poolside," Sylvie said.

Elba walked through the resort with her assistant manager, Pablo, and Charlie as they noted things that needed to be done for the day.

"You guys continue," Elba said, she paused at a large window that overlooked the back of the property. "Email your notes to me as soon as you're finished walking the grounds."

A couple of the guests entered the studio cabana.

Elba noted that they engaged the TV and queued it to yoga.

A few more were leaving with a local tour guide.

Jules swam laps in the newly renovated pool while Cassie walked leisurely on a treadmill in the gym.

Long Boy brought three horses to where a couple of tourists were waiting to go horseback riding.

Tears gathered in Elba's eyes, and she whispered silently, *Thank you for always sharing words of wisdom with me, Dad, and for teaching me everything I know about the resort. You wanted to keep this place going but didn't know how to deal with a more modern world. I hope you see your vision realized through me, and I hope I am doing the right things to advance us as a leader in the tourism industry. I promise to keep what you started going for a very long time.*

Elba took a deep breath and stepped away just as the sun rose above the canopy of trees, bathing the resort and surrounding areas in light.

"The promise of a new day," Kenny said behind her.

"Oh!" Elba turned quickly and stumbled.

Kenny's arms reached out and steadied her.

"Apologies, I didn't mean to sneak up on you," he said. "Sunrise is the favorite part of my day."

Kenny offered his arm. Elba slid her arms through his.

They walked in a moment of silence down the long hallway and reached the top of the stairs.

I didn't hesitate to take his arm. It happened quickly and felt good. That thought and a hint of a smile touched Elba's lips.

"The place is beautiful. The amenities are great," he said as they descended the stairway.

"I had quite a bit of renovations done at the end of last summer. Feedback is important. I always want to meet and exceed the expectations of my guests," Elba replied.

"The place does not disappoint," Kenny said. "Jules holds you in very high regard. I now see why. You ladies seem spiritually connected. It's nice to meet you, Elba Coconut."

"Aww, that makes me happy. I feel the same way about Jules. Thank you for the kind words."

"So, this is your first summer since the major improvements," Kenny said.

"Yup. I have some travelers booked here and there over the next five months and several groups, so it is good. I still have quite a few weeks available, though." Elba paused and hoped she wasn't oversharing.

"I was just telling, or rather emailing, a couple of my buddies back in South Carolina about this place. We're outdoor enthusiasts and newly retired. Anyway, you offer birdwatching along the river and tours to some Mayan monuments."

"Adventures and good experiences are what Belize is all about," Elba replied. She slid her arm from Kenny's and immediately missed his warmth.

"Adventure," Sam said as he walked toward Kenny and Elba. "This place seems to offer that in spades. I am getting a group of folks together, Elba. I think we'll be returning in a couple of months. I want to add cave explorations to my list as well. I saw it on your brochure."

"Good morning, guys." Jules strolled from the conference room where the others congregated and organized their space as they prepared for a few hours of *write-in*.

"Hi, Jules," Kenny said. "Sam and I were just sharing with Elba some plans to return on other trips with pals. This is a great place to stay, with creature comforts inside and the ability to explore the great outdoors."

Jules's brows arched excitedly for her friend. "That is awesome! I plan on putting together a few advertising ideas for Elba to consider."

"Oh, right. Jules offered to get some ads going in some parts of the States. I am excited to see what she will come up with."

After a few minutes, Elba excused herself to attend to her staff while the others retreated to the conference room to write.

"We only have one day left. I don't know where the time went," Kenny said to the group gathered around the swimming pool.

"Jules, you have to make this an annual event. I've accomplished so much in my novel. This place has just the right amount of fabulous," Cassie said, floating on her back and staring at the sky, the sun setting just over the mountain range.

"I'm in." "Me too. "I'm in too..." everyone in the group said excitedly.

"Alright, I understand!" Jules chuckled. "You're eager to return and explore my Belize!"

A few hours later, the night sky sparkled with bright, twinkling stars, and a full moon gently drifted in a clear stretch of space.

Elba maneuvered her SUV into the parking lot. The night fell silent again as she cut the engine.

Kenny spotted her from his bedroom window and quickly went downstairs. He stood under the dim lights of the canopy at the resort's entrance. He didn't want to startle her again, so he ensured she saw him.

Elba looked up and waved.

Kenny trotted toward her, wanting a moment of privacy before she entered the building.

"Hello again." Elba smiled.

"I was hoping I'd see you, Elba Coconut." Kenny's voice was husky.

"Oh, Jules won't go for that." She laughed.

"Okay, then—Elba Moon!" He tilted her head toward the moon overhead.

Elba laughed. "Good one. And now I must give you a name as well."

She looked around for a moment.

"Kenny Racoon!" She laughed.

"Say, what?" Kenny chuckled.

Elba pointed to the animal scurrying across the lawn.

"Perfect," Kenny replied.

"I want to thank you for making this week special," Kenny said, his arms looping before him.

"You're most welcome."

"Elba, I am going to kiss you," Kenny said.

"Yes?" she asked.

"One more thing—I am staying a bit longer."

"But your friends—"

"I will tell them that I'm lost in paradise."

Elba was about to respond just as his lips touched hers.

LOVE'S REMAINS

Deborah Hetrick Catanese

You may know it
or not –
when love may end.

You may seek it
yearn for it
have it only once
or again and again.

Your heart may ache
or burn
calm
or yearn
as you want it
again and again.

You will try to
obtain it
retain it
sustain it –
for naught.

Can you decide?
Will you reside
in love's unknown?
Or in fateful acceptance of its demise?

It doesn't matter, either way
you must face
this cursed certainty –
no matter how many times you
make love
take love
let love take you –
there will be a last time.

You can
try to use it
or abuse it.
Or choose it again and again.

You may go back
to soothe your parched need
to drink again from the holy chalice
to bask in the golden light
of their eyes reflecting your sunblast
of ephemeral satiation

In the end
it's all you've got –

that
Love's remains
remain
in you.

1st Place winner of Pennwriters' Poetry Contest, 2022.

CALL IN YOUR GHOSTS

Jennifer D. Diamond

The Waterfall of Your Mind

Blame Autumn for almost making you wreck the car. Blame it on the fall leaves set aflame by brilliant sunlight showering the world aglow.

On the way to your first writing retreat, your mind sprays erratically like a calcified shower head. What will you write this week? The column due later in the month? Social media posts promised as guest host of an online group? Or will you finally work on your own novella?

If those leaves weren't so flippin' gorgeous, you could pay attention to the road, but every curve of 711—the Pennsylvania state route, not the convenience store—dips into another valley where lemon-yellow weeping willows cascade over reflective ponds beside weathered barns adjacent to their well-kept century-old farmhouses, or the road rises to another vista where you want to pull over for an impromptu photo shoot of the rolling Laurel Highland Mountains bedazzled with candy-apple red maples, banana-peel silver birch, and toasted-toffee oaks. But you don't pull over because the new-ish-looking McMansion has signs posted at the end of its winding drive, "Private Property No Stopping No Turning." You wonder how much professional signs like that cost. You wonder how much their acres of post and rail fencing cost?

Dripping, spraying brain. Five days of writing time. So luxurious. *Hope the words flow easily.*

Now the road dips down through a hollow with a tiny stream running alongside a narrow road, cutting through thick pines and you think about turning there, to go back for the photo-op, but it's a dirt lane and it might actually be a driveway and you'd probably lock up the brakes, so with a glance in the rearview mirror you decide it's too risky with that SUV following so closely, and anyway by now you've reached the crest of another hilltop and somebody's going to think you're driving drunk! But you're not a big drinker. However, you *are* under the influence of your waterfall mind, taking in all the colors bombarding your senses.

Several more miles unfold with you "oohing" and "aahing" like a kid watching fireworks, reminding you of your favorite kind, fountains. And you're thinking about a bucket filled with sand for safely launching roman candles, which leads to you thinking about using a bucket to bail a leaky boat. But what if the bucket leaks, too?

The River of Your Mind

Burgundy maples line both sides of the lane along the long driveway leading up the hill to the lodge perched high above a little and historic, but regal and bustling, town. The trees seem to greet all guests passing between them, so you reply, "Well, hello there!" And you imagine if you weren't currently driving you might bow at the feet of these grand trees.

Stepping out of the air-conditioned car into the bonus-summer-in-October heat, you hold your hand over your brow, taking in the valley stretched out before you. Intense harvest sunrays warm your bare arms and legs as you unload and carry a week's worth of gear to the retreat lodge lobby. Once directed to your room, you find beautiful gifts. One box holds a labradorite and leather necklace, with a note explaining how the stone is believed to amplify intuition, creativity, and inspire transformation. A suede-covered notebook begs to be touched, opened, written upon with the gold pen or maybe the Blackwing pencil. You feel like you've stepped into the world of proper writers. The busywork of setting up your writing spot can't be finished quickly enough, yet maybe you're procrastinating from the real reason you're here—to write.

Now, the Mindful Writers Retreat attendees sit in a circle in front of an unlit fireplace in the gathering room of the lodge. Your heart skips beats because the thought of telling these immensely talented writers about your writing goal for the week squeezes your stomach and tightens your throat. *Am I a real writer?* The mean voice in your head questions your motives and makes you feel small, and you'd tell it to shut up if only you could pay attention long enough to silence it. But you don't notice the river of your mind rushing over enormous boulders, white water roughing the surface. Mostly you're noticing the sweat under your shirt and the discomfort in the small of your back and the tightness in your jaw and the way your palms feel sticky resting on the tops of your thighs just below the hem of your shorts while *trying* to listen to each person speaking.

A lit bay leaf candle helps you silently set your intentions. Then a small Bluetooth speaker is cued, signaling time for group meditation. This guided meditation is one of your favorites. You could recite it word for word. Since this is your first group meditation, you're not sure how different it's going to feel from your solo practice in the comfort of home. Will extraneous noises bother you? Will you feel self-conscious sitting with your eyes closed? Are you holding your hands in the correct position? Are you messing it up? But thankfully you fall into the narrator's voice, and everything else dissipates. Energy flows from every pore in your body, while at the same time it mingles with that of your fellow meditators, resonating throughout the room. Once the meditation ends, everyone moves silently to their writing spots.

While the idea of only-writing-all-day for five straight days sounds like a grand privilege, and it is, when you sit at your keyboard, your fingers hover. You *think* you know what you want to write. How do you get started?

"Begin with the action," you were once taught.

Okay, I'll start there.

And then. And, well. And. And, and, and... nothing. Words? Where are the words? *Just start.* So, you type a few lines, then immediately backspace. A peculiar cha-cha ensues—two words forward, two words deleted. You sigh. Lean back in your chair. Stare blankly out the window at the little tree below your windowsill, appreciating its deep-garnet foliage.

At dinner, the mood is bright, welcoming and friendly. One writer asks you about your progress. You begin by explaining how your late mother dreamed of becoming a writer but died suddenly of a heart attack before she could, so you'd started writing to honor her dream.

The writer looks over your shoulder and says, "Your mother is standing right behind you."

Goosebumps raise the hairs on your arms and the chill runs up the back of your neck, and then, to your dismay, you're crying. Joyous tears stream down your face, and you swipe at them with the back of your hand as they roll off the end of your chin. She apologizes for making you cry. The whole encounter caught you off-guard, but you're grateful. You thank her and hug like you've known each other forever.

Walking the path from the dining hall to the lodge, you're struck with awe at the tangerine clouds hanging so low, you jump, trying to touch them. A large group gathers, but the boisterous chatter hushes, softens as the mountains usher the sun toward setting. Then, what began as dewy fog low in the valley, rises like a gauzy sheet pulled up from the creek bed as the blood-orange ball disappears. Tranquility envelops you as angled sunrays streak across the sky. On gray winter days, you'll conjure every detail of this moment to remember how light always wins over darkness.

Then, your next exhale is a strident, "Oh!" because right at eye level, on the opposite ridgeline, a faint rainbow forms.

The woman beside you crouches low, whispering, coaxing the rainbow to fully show itself. "Come on, baby. Come on, now. You can do it."

And her voice gets louder as she stands, raising her hands, and the rainbow deepens to a vibrancy you haven't experienced in years. Would kneeling in the gravel, lowering yourself into child's pose and then back up again be too much? Not with darned shorts and bare knees.

Though rainbows genuinely deserve genuflecting, don't they? Yes, even the lawn-sprinkler rainbows you'd leapt through as a kid and the backyard-garden-hose rainbows you'd made by pressing your thumb against the flow of water.

The Ice Jam of Your Mind

Frozen bodies of water give the illusion of solid ground, appearing like snow-covered fields. In the town where you grew up, a seasoned trucker or two who'd lost their brakes careened out of control down the mile-long hill with a ten percent downgrade. But without a crash-ramp, how would they manage? How exhausting it must be to haul America's necessities. How horrifying it must have been to lose control, barreling ever faster down the hill. If they weren't familiar with the terrain, a frozen river at the bottom lured them onto thin ice with its snowy meadow disguise. It must've been even more terrifying for those truckers who knew the area, because they understood their only option was to muscle their eighteen-wheeler through a ninety-degree turn in the road, knowing they'd end up slamming into a little white house in the exact wrong, or right spot, depending on your perspective. They probably knew about other truckers who had made the same attempt and smashed the side of the small but quaint two-story dwelling only to have it rebuilt, only to have it crashed into again a few years later. But what other choice did they have? On the other hand, those newbie-first-timers might have felt relieved as they cruised straight ahead, avoiding the treacherous turn, trading it for another peril. Unfortunately, they'd been mesmerized by the frozen mirage of glistening ice, taking it as a narrow pasture covered in snow. They paid a dear price for taking the illusion at its seemingly solid surface.

These are the strange thoughts rushing through your raging river mind, even though you sit motionless. You stare at the incessant blinking cursor with your rigid body giving the illusion of stillness, like the illusion of the river during that hard mid-winter freeze. Authentic stillness requires ease, but under your frozen layers, thoughts rumble over rocks and carry snapped trees along as playthings where they occasionally tap on the underside of the ice, thinking they can break through and escape. But the only escape is to acknowledge the rough waters and what lies in their deepest depths. Ignoring your stiff, locked muscles will eventually cause the heavy load on the bed of your tractor trailer to break through the ice, pulling you into the frigid water. There you'll remain a frozen block. This image of doom sends shivers of itchy restlessness through every muscle. The remedy requires a walk outside.

The night sky above the retreat center has opened, revealing a million celestial twinkle-lights. The air is crisp, tinted with wood smoke from the great room fireplace. To the west, a faraway flash brings to mind a back-home expression—heat lightning—though it's not hot anymore because without the sun, coolness rushes toward frosty in a frenzied hurry. Still in your shorts, you walk fast to get some blood pumping. Motion is the lotion, and not just for your muscles. Walking lubes your squeaking brain gears, too, so even though it's chilly, you pace the driveway in front of the lodge until you're struck by an idea. Run the staircase two steps at a time. Burst into your room. Grab your notebook to write this tidbit of hopefulness before it escapes, or worse, gets lost in the slushy mush of your jammed river mind.

The Underground River of Your Mind

When you were a small child, your father gently tucked in you and your sister at night with a bedtime story. Some were real. Some contained ghosts. And some had fantastical fictional elements while still rooted in snippets of truth. To the younger sister who'd been called "gullible" more times than she could count, his tale of a mysterious underground river flowing beneath their town felt fake, yet magical. But this twin river aquifer actually exists. Deep within a vein of porous limestone, naturally purified water flows, perfect for drinking, watering gardens, or filling swimming pools in summer. This bedrock filters impurities, so no one has to deal with them. Eventually, though, the water bubbles to the surface. If not dealt with, your cellar floods, and once it recedes, could fester mold or other nastiness, sure to wreak havoc on all levels. Whether your father's stories were fact, fiction, or somewhere in between, when he finished telling them, he would sit on the front porch to have one last cigarette before turning in for the night. In warmer months, the smell of his Marlboro Lights wafted through your open window as you drifted off sleep.

During your first night at the retreat camp and conference center, subterranean fears stalk you. A shadow who occasionally surfaces in your dreams comes out to play. The only light in your dorm-like, bunkbed-filled room streams under your locked door from the hallway. In the dimness, an abysmal outline in the shape of tiny human shoulders with an oversized head hovers at the foot of your bunk. You scream, but no one in your dreamworld is near enough to hear.

Lucidity creeps in; your mind begins to understand you're dreaming. *Wake up!* But you won't wake up. The head tilts right, then slowly left, observing, studying. *No!* you scream, but your mouth won't open. A lamp on the small table beside your mattress sits within reach, if only your arm would move. Looking at the lamp, pleading for your body to obey, pretending the shadow has gone, doesn't help. When the bed shakes like someone's trying to move it, you look back at the shadow as it liquifies, losing all resemblance to anything human.

With your heart hammering, you scream again, making grunting sounds through super-glued lips. The oily mass slithers through the slats of the makeshift ladder and presses on your feet. You kick and thrash and scream and curse, but paralyzed bodies won't do any of those things. Squeezing your eyes shut and holding your breath are the only actions you have any volition over. *You're dreaming; it's just a dream. This is not real.* Things said when comforting a child during his nightmares. Like a demented lead blanket being pulled from the bottom of the bed, the heaviness presses its way up to your chest. When you open your eyes, there's complete blackness. No light coming under the door. No light faintly seeping through the curtains. No light inside you. The weight threatens to crush your ribs. Your lungs burn for oxygen. *I'm dying.* An image of kicking a bucket flashes. Your leg bangs the wall, and you wake up sweating, pulse racing, breathing and alive.

Can a dented, leaking bucket ever overflow?

In the morning, breakfast conversation centers on the previous night's wicked thunderstorm. How the thunder and lightning didn't wake you is perplexing. While telling a few people about your strange night terror, one of them says, "That's just your soul, and all the souls of your ancestors, trying to re-enter your body."

"Huh," you say.

Never had you heard such an optimistic explanation of night terrors, and you're grateful.

Outside, cold drizzle and stiff breezes prove the demise of false summer, which usually means a happy excuse to write all day. But the loss of fall foliage creates a melancholy sensation. The little maple outside your window looks barren, naked, so you stare at the woods further behind the lodge. Placing your fingers on the keyboard feels like doing something, but nothing happens… feels like it never will. So, you stand, stretch, lie on your yoga mat, get a snack, and sit down with pen and paper. But even after doodling, words remain elusive. Another walk is called for, rainy or not.

Rain gear and galoshes replace the previous day's shorts and tennis shoes. Freshly fallen leaves blanket woodsy trails with smells only October releases. The ancient oaks alone hold on to their autumn adornments. Off trail, you sit on a tree stump with eyes closed, listening to the tick-tick-tick of raindrops bouncing off nature's brown trampolines. Magical energy flows through your body, and you're suddenly fully awake for what feels like the first time, so you head back toward the lodge, hoping you'll see the fruits of this walk in the form of words pouring onto the page.

Along the way, tucked in the trees, caddy-corner behind the lodge, you come upon a large barn-like pavilion with a full-sized basketball court, regulation hoops and all, with an outdoor fireplace at one end. Curious, you go to check it out and inadvertently interrupt the rainbow-coaxing woman from your retreat. She's sitting on the hearthstone curled over a notebook with her hair covering her face. You try not to bother her, but she notices you. So, you get to chatting and she says, "You know, I can't write in the big lodge because it's too noisy."

"How do you mean?" you ask, because so far, the lodge is exceedingly quiet when everyone's writing.

"It's because writers call in their loved ones to help them write."

Her hands cover her ears.

"And these people all talk to me—the dead ones, I mean."

Now her head is shaking, and her fingers are wriggling, and you feel the clammer and racket she must endure. "They want me to tell you what they're saying, and I want to help, really I do, but I've come here to get my own writing done, and I just can't do it with everyone's ghosts vying for my attention."

She looks up at you. "You're sensitive, too, aren't you?"

"I don't know," you say, because you don't know how to respond.

"It's a gift. Many writers have it, but they don't know how to listen."

"Huh," you say, noncommittally.

"Use it," she says with conviction. "It'll make you stronger."

"Thanks," you say.

And it's as if a salve has sealed your leaking bucket. Will its contents be fluid or frozen?

The Release of Your Mind

Back at your laptop again, you sit. Still. Eyes closed. You sit *with* stillness. Thoughts keep going back to the moment you were told your late mother stood behind you in the cafeteria—the feeling of it, the goosebumps and release of emotions. You count your breaths. Thoughts about when the woman under the basketball pavilion looked you straight in the eyes and said, "You're sensitive."

Then you hear a voice say, *You're strong.*

And like a tap on a block of ice with a sharpened pick, a slurry breaks loose, unleashing zings of energy down your arms, through your hands. The voice tells you what to write. Does this make you strange to have a stranger's voice in your head?

Who cares if you're strange?

"Not me!"

No one's opinion matters. Not even those of your ghosts. Call them. Listen. But you have the final say. Reassurance resides in acceptance and renewing your story bucket requires regular outpouring. Time to stop drowning in stagnant waters.

The Lake of Your Mind

A river backchannels as it empties into a larger body of water. Allow the swirling for a little while but remind yourself how treading water for too long leads to exhaustion. Ultimately, learning the Deadman's Float may be the best available lifesaver, even though lifting your head to breathe without expending too much energy involves continual practice.

That night, a comforting, recurring dream plays out— from your childhood bed, your mother opens the bedroom door to check on you, like she always did. Then, you're awake in your retreat room. Sensations of movement come from the corner. But there's no fear. No sense of danger or dread. Just a presence. After reciting a prayer, sleep returns, but again and again, the process repeats. Dream. Shuffling sounds. Slight movements in the shadows. Prayers. Sleep. Waking. Finally, you say, "Thanks for helping, but I can't write when I'm sleep deprived!"

And for the rest of the retreat, with eyes closed, your fingertips fly over the keyboard while a disembodied voice dictates the story with an otherworldly energy.

On the drive home, the scent of cigarettes forms inside your car.

"Thanks, Dad," you say. "But I'm good."

AN APOLOGY IN BLOOM

Hilary Hauck

Day One

"**S**ometimes, you wake up and find you no longer recognize the person you've dedicated a lifetime of love to."

Jasmine had arrived at her solo retreat with this opening line, her battered red leather journal, and every intention of writing the first draft of a story to launch her second career built on apologies.

Her first career had been *The Forget-Me-Not Shop* where she had harvested the best 'sorries', snippets of excuses plucked from her customers, the buds of ideas she would begin to this week. It was her long-awaited return to fiction—a solo retreat in a two-thousand-year-old town, nestled in the Italian countryside, an apartment to herself. She was all set.

She wiped the breakfast crumbs from the table and set out a notebook, three freshly sharpened pencils, and her red journal.

Trust that the story that needs to be written will come to you. That's what she had learned years earlier at a retreat in the Laurel Highlands, the seeds of that story no doubt sewn in the pages of her journal.

She had no illusions of becoming a bestseller, but she had owned her own business for decades and had a good sense of building and maintaining a loyal following. Readers who loved flowers and short stories—a niche audience. Jasmine just needed to cultivate her writing skills and pluck from her basket of marketing skills. She could see no reason why her new career wouldn't bloom in no time.

The prompt for her first story was a grandmother apologizing for her husband's refusal to acknowledge their grandchild's preferred gender. So much emotion here. She could recall the woman's insistence on picking out just the right flowers for her grandchild she still knew so intimately, without it mattering a stitch if the child were Harry or Harriet, and her despair at having spent her entire life with a man who shunned their grandchild because he couldn't imagine a truth that did not match his own.

On the first page, Jasmine had written her opening line. On the second page, with the title Journey to Retreat, she had written George Woodbury in large letters.

Ah that. It had slipped her mind after the fatigue of an Atlantic flight.

The strangest start to her retreat. The odds of the boarding pass she had found left in one of those airport check-in machines in—of all the 8 billion people on the planet—the name of her first love. Such an unexpected twist.

She turned over the page and wrote *Day One*.

'A grandmother mortified. Apologizing for husband cutting ties with granddaughter, formerly grandson. High emotions. Grandmother's despair.'

Jasmine closed her eyes and pictured the grandmother standing over her granddaughter, admiring what might well have been her first ever gift of flowers. In the background, an old man looked on. He wore jeans and a buttoned shirt. Gray curly hair. His face a scowl, blue eyes, freckles—an older version of George.

Jasmine's mind was playing tricks on her. She was only thinking of George because of the boarding pass. At the time, she had looked around the airport, just in case, but he hadn't even been interested in travel back then, and she certainly had no reason to expect he lived anywhere near her in Pittsburgh.

At any rate, she could never imagine George would be anything but loving and supportive to his grandchildren, if he had any. She hoped he had.

She forced a new image of the grandfather's face in her story. Terry, she'd call him. Brown eyes, pallid, drooping skin. Left alone in what should have been his golden years, if only his heart hadn't been so full of hate.

Day Two

After breakfast, Jasmine reread what she had written the day before. An entire day, and only two pages to show for it. Two very poorly written pages, as it turned out. She put it down to jetlag and the bottle of Assisi Rosso she'd opened mid-afternoon.

Or perhaps the story was too ambitious for her long-awaited return to writing. Perhaps it needed to be story number two or three. But also, she hadn't worked all those years in the flower shop to write a story that couldn't have a happy ending.

At that retreat years ago, with writers who knew what they were doing, they had walked in the woods every morning, channeling characters and plot points.

They had told her to take her characters with her. If her mind wandered, to focus back on body, breath, book. It had sounded odd at first but it worked surprisingly well. No harm in substituting the woods for the ancient cobbled streets of Assisi.

Jasmine put her shoes on and turned uphill out of the apartment; so far, she had not found a single level street in Assisi. The apartment was on a side street, lined by what seemed to be residential buildings as opposed to shops and businesses. Fewer distractions.

She stopped for a moment to admire a balcony dripping with flowers. Just past the balcony was an even narrower street. She stopped in her tracks. At the other end she saw a man. About her height, wearing a blue bomber jacket, jeans, and black curly hair. Uncanny. Just like George.

This was becoming surreal. She felt a little giddy as she walked toward him.

She couldn't catch up before he turned onto the next street and became lost to the crowd, or perhaps to one of the little shops. She had to at least try. She dodged in between the pedestrians, who filled the width of the street until a car approached from behind, going perhaps not at top speed, but certainly faster than seemed wise. Jasmine had no choice but to step to the side with everyone else until it passed.

Minutes later, she walked through an archway and into an open square filled with tour buses. No George.

Jasmine shook her head. What on earth was she allowing to go through her mind? The man resembled and dressed like George thirty years ago. The same aging process that had streaked her hair and broadened her body would have aged him, too. The person she had seen could not possibly have been George. Besides, what would he be doing all the way over here in Italy? In the very same town at the very same time she was here? No. Again, he was only on her mind because of the boarding pass.

She turned and retraced her steps, trying to block out the bustle around her. Body, breath, book. Or short story, in her case. But if she wasn't going to write about the hostile grandfather, she still had to figure out which story would be her first. What about the three-dozen daisies man?

Jasmine remembered telling him that daisies could signify a fresh start or a break, but he had not indulged her with the reason for his purchase. So, she would make it up.

She pictured him now, ready to present his bouquet and floral request for a fresh start. Her freedom as author gave her the right to choose. An oversized yellow sofa, white cushions. Yes, that's it, the room color coordinated with the blooms. Some framed photos hanging on the wall.

A plant in the corner, a dracaena—no, a ficus. Textured cream curtains, a woman on the sofa, in tears, and the man in the doorway, unseen by the crying girlfriend, contemplating the wrong he'd done to her, and whether he would take responsibility or walk away. A solid start to the story.

Back at the apartment, she inhaled deeply. Flexing her shoulders, she put her fingers to the keyboard and started typing. Only now, that clear image of the living room scrambled in her mind. A hazy sofa, the curtains—some kind of textured pattern. The man by the sofa clearly George again.

She huffed and typed, 'Timothy has realized he accepts his girlfriend for exactly who she is—' gosh, wasn't that every woman's dream? And yet, wasn't that what George had done to her? 'Timothy,' she underlined, 'had gray eyes and blond hair.' She forced word after word onto the screen.

But any hint of excitement stemmed from seeing the white space disappear, not because of her actual words. As she forced brown-eyed Timothy into the story, the colors of the living room dulled and her words droned until they depicted a scene devoid of interest even to her.

As pointless as it seemed, she kept going. She remembered the importance of getting words on the page. A story wasn't that dissimilar to a bouquet. You could rearrange words and flowers until you found the most cohesive or attention-grabbing arrangement.

Day Three

The next morning, Jasmine forced down her coffee (why did espresso made in a moka pot taste so bitter when it tasted so good at a café?) and a croissant, a little crumbly now that it wasn't fresh. She stared at the wall. Perhaps if she allowed herself to think about George, he wouldn't intrude on her story later.

She'd been dating someone else when she opened the shop, blown him off because of her new busy schedule. She'd never looked back and never felt guilty about him, sensing the feeling might be mutual.

George though, he came earlier, when she still felt so confused about life. About how everyone else seemed to have their act together when on the inside, she was a train wreck. Not a time she liked to remember.

Writing would be a welcome distraction. She couldn't bring herself to reread the previous day's draft, but she had another idea. A story without a man in it, about a bouquet a woman had spent ample time putting together, hoping her girlfriend would be able to decode the message of each flower. Jasmine had enjoyed it, she appreciated someone actually paying attention to the meaning of flowers.

The woman had begun with hydrangeas for heartfelt emotions and gratitude. Yet they could also mean understanding. George would not have understood her sudden disappearance.

How about a spray of freesias instead? They stood for trust and friendship. George had trusted her, and they had both considered each other as best friends.

Scrap all that. Orchids were the way to go, signifying admiration and commitment. A commitment she'd broken to George when she had ignored his phone calls.

Anemones stand for abiding love. It wasn't so much that her love had stopped abiding, rather that she could not love the woman he loved—the broken her.

This story was clearly going nowhere.

Day Four

Still a world away from having anything coherent on paper, Jasmine spent the entire morning doodling flowers in her notebook.

How about the man clutching the apology of a dozen roses as though they were a prayer book? He had practiced the lines he would say to his wife, not caring that Jasmine heard him.

Of course, he hadn't really said anything out loud, but Jasmine was amused by this version of the story.

Then again, roses were such a cliché. No imagination. She went back to doodling.

At midday, she decided to eat out for lunch and, while she was out, pick up some fresh bread.

She found a darling outdoor table at a gem of a restaurant at the end of an alley. She people-watched over a divine meal of tagliatelle with truffles, washed down with a good glass of red. When in Rome—or Assisi—why not round off lunch with a pistachio gelato? She would eat it and indulge in some window shopping to gather inspiration.

In a clothing store window, she chose an elegant black dress for a main character—she liked the idea of the story being about a woman. The shoe shop next door gave her a perfect pair of flats. She crossed over to look in a jeweler's shop window for accessories to complete her character's outfit.

Jasmine selected drop pearl earrings. She glanced over some silver necklaces so quickly she almost didn't notice—in pride of place—a necklace with a quarter, or rather, half a quarter for a pendant, a jagged line where it had been cut in two.

She almost dropped her ice cream. It could have been the very same necklace George had given her years earlier. The one he had had made with the quarter he saved from a childhood trip to California. He had presented his half of the coin to her with the promise that he would always keep the other half, no matter where she was. That the two sides would always fit perfectly together, just like he and she would. Or so he had thought.

By the time Jasmine reached her apartment, she had failed horribly at holding back the tears.

The memories she had suppressed all these years. The man who had been kinder than anyone to her, years before she had been able to do the same. How had she been so cruel to him?

Day Five

She lay in bed, uninspired to move, thinking about George.

His 'crime' in their relationship had been to accept her for who she was at a time when she was unable to accept herself. Deep down, she had known that if she continued to lean on him, she would never hold herself accountable and fix the mess inside her, the darkness that drove her to dare anyone close to reject her, because she was nothing. She was invisible. Yet try as she had, he had never rejected her.

It had taken her years to pull herself up by the bootstraps. To grow some self-esteem. And she had paid a hefty price in opportunities missed, scrambling to weave a career after dropping out of college.

Did he even know she was sorry, that she knew it was *her* fault, not his? That she regretted the way she had hurt him?

She would never get a chance to tell him. She had no idea where he lived.

Maybe if she could find a way to track down his address, she could send flowers out of the blue. An apology thirty years too late. But utterly damaging if he was married.

And would fate ever allow her to randomly cross paths with him? She could just walk up to him and say sorry—

also would not go down well if he happened to be with, say, his wife.

All these thoughts were opening an old wound. It had taken years to brush aside her guilt for leaving George.

But then, she had paid off a little guilt with every bouquet she painstakingly arranged for others who were also paying the price. Wrapped them in cream and blush tissue paper, and styled every curl of her handwriting with sincerity on the note.

Over time, accepting a sliver of guilt belonging to those she helped had grown her into a better version of herself. She had scattered her remorse for every dumb word she had said, every deed she had done wrong, every person she had hurt, alongside her customers', until she had pruned away the thorns of her previous self.

She forced herself to get up and make coffee but took it back to bed. She relished its bitterness. It was what she deserved.

This week had turned into a reckoning of past failures rather than the retreat she'd intended. So much for finding the story she was meant to write. She was finding, instead, that she wasn't meant to write at all.

After a lunch of a cheese rind (still no bread) and an over-ripe plum, she dragged her chair to the window, searching the narrow road for a hint of the excitement and confidence she'd arrived with.

In the shower, she gave herself a last-ditch pep talk about not having got to where she was by giving up so easily. It was almost the final day and all she had was a series of false starts, superficial stories, and a weight-load of regret.

Shaking off the despair, she rifled through the pages of story prompts one more time.

A man (men normally had more apologizing to do) who expected flowers to make his girlfriend forget about his recent absence. But, of course, the story soon morphed into a girl who had ghosted her boyfriend, for reasons that had nothing to do with him, and everything to do with her own state of mind.

It was no good. No matter how many stories Jasmine looked at in her red leather journal, every one of them was bound to lead back to George.

During her 'dinner' of plums and apricots, washed down by slightly more than half a bottle of wine, she decided it was time to call it quits. Writing was not, after all, for her. She could at least spend the day doing what everyone else did in Assisi—being a tourist.

Two basilicas, the church St. Francis of Assisi restored, wine tasting—she had plenty to do.

Day Six

Jasmine woke to church bells, well before her alarm. Had they rung every morning?

She pushed back the covers and let her feet fall to the floor. The cold tile enhanced the clarity she had woken with. She welcomed the bells as a celebratory backdrop for the apparition of a story that flooded her mind all at once in surprising detail. How could she not have thought of it before?

She didn't waste time getting dressed. She downed her coffee in her pajamas, brushing aside its bitterness as a temporary annoyance. The important thing was the jolt of caffeine she needed to set down the story she was clearly meant to write.

She cleared off the kitchen table and opened her computer. Certainly not the story she had ever wanted to write, but for certain the one she *needed* to write. She owed it to George, and she owed it to herself. After, perhaps, she could begin to truly forgive herself.

"Sometimes," she wrote, "a great love arrives too soon, before one of the two—the girl, in this case—has learned to love herself."

Retreating Within the Silence

Judy England–McCarthy

Nature
    Surrounds me, in the dead of winter, I sit and wait.

My **words** find their rhythmic dance
                       Stepping
            onto

        the page.
        Joining, whirling, and
        moving to the beat of my soul.

I close my eyes to draw them out.
I retreat into the silence.
           It seeps in.

     Ideas begin to arise, they percolate
     and b
        u
         b
        b
          le out,

I reach for them before they can
Return from where they came.

The vast space...
                                    of emptiness.
                        Retreating Within the Silence

Words

        fall onto the page

The   space   between the words grows
                                    Expanding

                        and
                    contracting

I begin to see,
The cosmic dance.

Retreating deeper,
my voice sings out its melody.

As silence
            Seeps in,
                    steeping me,
in its endless pot of awareness.

Free-floating in the ocean of limitlessness

Desire to control dissolves with each breath
I find home here.
No longer lost,

Within the presence of my awareness,
My endless thoughts

> ill-fitting shoes, uncomfortable to tread on
> fade away, worn and useless.

Their journey was aimless, ill-formed, and without understanding.

In bare feet, I tread in the sands of countless deserts

Each grain is a different universe.

Encompassed by **space**

What is and always was permeates my being,

I am no longer adrift

Home at last.

The lost child within me settles,
comforted by returning to
A mother's enduring embrace.

The more I reside away from my structured views
It reminds me, I was never alone.

A CERTAIN MAGIC

Phil Giunta

Why was this place so familiar? Keri Lange had never been to Ligonier, Pennsylvania, before the previous afternoon and yet, she'd been haunted by a relentless feeling of déjà vu from the moment she arrived.

Keri paused along the trail as the first rays of the rising sun highlighted the resplendent autumn colors of the surrounding trees. Her gaze swept across the expansive field of green and brown grass bordered by a narrow, meandering creek on its north side and Macartney Lane to the south. Beyond the far edge of the field, opposite the trail on which she stood, sparse traffic flowed along Route 711.

Macartney Lane was the only road in or out of the Ligonier Camp and Conference Center, her home for the next four days. Nestled in the Laurel Highlands region of the Allegheny Mountains, the 500-acre property was a summer camp for kids, but a group of writers from the nearby Pittsburgh area rented the place for a weeklong retreat every October. It was the perfect location to break away from life and get into the creative flow all while nestled in the bosom of Mother Nature. Although Keri lived several hours away, she'd connected with a few of the local writers at a recent conference and was invited to join them.

One of the first things she'd learned during orientation was that many of the writers took sunrise walks to clear their minds before immersing themselves in their work. For Keri, it was a welcome change of pace from the stress of urban life.

To her right, a path of dirt and stone wound its way up to the distant crest of a hill. Keri was tempted to make the climb but she'd been walking for over an hour and her stomach was grumbling. She made a mental note to tackle the hill the next day and continued along the trail until she arrived at Macartney Lane. There, a large wooden sign served as an information marker about the Wilpen train crash that had occurred a few hundred yards away on July 5, 1912. The trail on which she'd been walking had once been a branch of the Ligonier Valley Railroad and the site of a horrific collision between a passenger train headed north to Wilpen and a freight train carrying coal on its way south to Ligonier on the same track. Twenty-seven people were killed and twenty-six injured.

Overcome with inexplicable dread, Keri backed away from the sign and darted up the road to the lodge as if some calamity might befall her if she lingered too long.

The rest of the morning passed without further apprehension. Seated against a window in the first-floor lounge, Keri had become so absorbed in her writing that it was almost lunch time when she glanced up from her laptop. Contemplating the next scene in her story, she stared out at the grassy hill behind the lodge and the tree line beyond—until the blast of a train whistle jolted her. She glanced around the room at the other writers, but none of them appeared disturbed by the sound, even when it happened again.

Maybe they're used to it, since most of them have been here before. But I thought the railroad was long gone. A brief Google search confirmed that it had been decommissioned in 1952. *So where did that whistle come from? It was so close!*

Keri was tempted to dash outside and track it down until retreat organizers Carla Poole and Barry Sharpe gathered with two other writers and started toward the back door.

Carla leaned toward her as she sauntered past. "Comin' to lunch?"

Keri closed the lid on her laptop and joined them as they made their way out of the lodge and up the hill to the cafeteria building. "Did any of you hear a train whistle a few minutes ago?"

"Train whistle?" Carla shook her head. "Nope. I don't think any trains run through this area."

"The lodge offices are just down the hall from us," Barry said. "Maybe one of their computers makes a train whistle sound when an email comes in or an alert pops up."

Keri shrugged. "I guess that makes sense."

"How's your writing going?" Carla asked.

"I'm one scene away from finishing this reincarnation story I started last week. It's about a woman who travels back to her previous life in order to rescue someone and change history. I was struggling with the ending, but this morning's walk helped clear my mind."

"That's what this retreat's all about," Barry said. "There's a certain magic here. The guided meditations we do after lunch should help you stay in the creative flow and knock out that last scene."

"That's the plan. Once the story's done, I can give it a quick edit and send it to my critique partners."

"You still have three days left," Carla said. "Got anything else?"

"I could work on a novella I put aside a few months ago," Keri replied. "Unless I get an idea for something new. I see there was a train crash here back in 1912. Maybe I'll research that. Might get a story idea out of it."

"That happened two years before this camp was founded." Barry opened the door and motioned for the women to precede him into the cafeteria. "We've had enough strange occurrences here over the years to wonder if this place is haunted by some of the people who died in that crash."

Keri recalled her unsettling experience on the trail. "That... would explain a lot."

"Close your eyes, plant your feet firmly on the ground with your palms on your thighs."

Backed by soft music, the soothing voice of the instructor drifted from the Bluetooth speaker in the middle of the room as the guided meditation began. *"Start by breathing in and out slowly three times..."*

"It's so humid out here, I can hardly breathe at all."

What?

Keri opened her eyes and winced at the blinding afternoon sun. Trickles of sweat ran down the sides of her face. She adjusted her glasses and stepped back under the shade of the train station roof.

Glasses? Train station? Where the hell—?

At least fifty people crowded the platform, all of them dressed in clothing from the early twentieth century. At two quick tugs on her skirt, Keri peered down at a girl no more than six years old, dirty blonde hair matted to her forehead.

"Ms. Matthews, when's the train coming?"

"What? Oh, uh..." Keri stammered. "I'm sure it'll be here soon, Sarah." *How did I know her name?*

"Four minutes, to be exact."

The plump middle-aged man beside her held up his pocket watch and smiled. "It's almost never late, Esther. You should know that better than anyone. You work for the railroad." A white suit jacket was slung over his opposite shoulder. It matched his pleated white pants and waistcoat. The sleeves of his light blue shirt were rolled up, armpits drenched in sweat.

How did people survive summers in these outfits?

"Right... of course. Four minutes." Keri put a gentle hand on the girl's shoulder and leaned down. "Four minutes, sweetie."

"Billie and Bernadetta won't stop fighting and I think Elizabeth is gonna faint from the heat."

Keri looked past her at the four girls sitting on the concrete floor in the middle of the platform. *Good God, are all of them mine?*

"Mighty nice of you to take the kids out while their parents are workin'," the man said.

Sarah beamed. "We're gonna pick wildflowers up at Mill Creek."

"Is that right? Well, that sounds like a pleasant way to spend a summer afternoon."

"I better check on the others." Holding Sarah's hand, Keri scurried over to the gaggle of squirming youngsters. Towering over them, a man in soot-stained overalls folded back the front page of a newspaper to read the bottom half. Keri caught sight of the date.

July 5, 1912.

Wait, wasn't that when—

She whirled at the screech of a train whistle followed by the slow trundling of wheels along the track. Four of the kids cheered and dashed toward the edge of the platform. The oldest one, Elizabeth, lagged behind and gulped water from a metal canteen.

"Be careful!" Keri darted ahead of them and spread her arms. "Don't want you falling off."

A young woman in a white linen dress scurried over to help. "You're gonna have your hands full today, Esther. Good luck in this heat."

Two of the girls waved at her. "Hi, Besse!"

"Hi, Elizabeth. Hi, Sarah. You all listen to Ms. Matthews today, okay? Don't give her any guff."

Keri had never seen a train travel backwards before, but this one did. It consisted of a single passenger car being pushed by a steam engine. Once it came to a stop, the engineer hopped out and yelled, "All aboard!"

She ushered the children ahead of her into the passenger car. The six of them took up two rows of seats along the left side. By the time everyone filed in, every seat was full and the stench of body odor became nauseating. Keri clenched her jaw against the urge to retch and was never more grateful for a window seat.

A familiar, soft voice rose above the din. *"Now cross your arms and grip each shoulder with the opposite hand."*

Keri turned away from the open window. The passengers were gone, as was the interior of the train. She was back in the lodge, surrounded once again by her fellow writers.

"Hold yourself in a tight, warm embrace," the instructor continued. *"Breathe in... and breathe out..."*

A few minutes later, the guided meditation concluded and Keri was at her laptop searching the name Esther Matthews. She found a few websites that referenced the Ligonier Valley Railroad and the Wilpen train wreck. There was little information on Esther. She had been a nurse employed by the railroad and on July 5, 1912, she was to escort five children to Wilpen to pick wildflowers along Mill Creek. None of them survived the crash.

So why did I have a vision as if I were Esther? Maybe this land is haunted, like Barry said, and she's trying to get a message to me. Or could I have been Esther in a past life? I have three more days to figure this out and something tells me she isn't done with me yet.

The following morning saw the camp shrouded in dense fog. Lamp posts and the exterior lights of buildings were little more than faint orbs surrounded by hazy auras of pale green and yellow. In the still air, the trees stood as menacing silhouettes against a gray sky. Distant mountains, majestic in the light of day, were all but invisible.

From the window of Keri's room, Macartney Lane vanished about twenty feet down the hill. *Maybe I'll try the trail behind the lodge this time.* She laced up her hiking boots, slipped on her jacket, and grabbed the LED lantern that had been a welcome gift from Carla. She'd bought one for every attendee, along with a coffee mug, pencils, pens, and other goodies.

Downstairs, Keri found the lounge devoid of life. From her table by the window, she expected to see some activity outside—shadowy forms, other lanterns bobbing in the fog—but there was no movement at all. It was only a few minutes after 7:00. Was she the last one to wake up? Was everyone else already well into the woods or down by the creek?

Keri crept outside through the back door, careful not to let it slam behind her lest she disturb the unnatural peace. Even the birds were quiet, if there were any birds around. Keri pressed her back to the door, overwhelmed by the same trepidation she'd felt the day before while walking along the trail at the bottom of the hill. *I'm not going down there this time. I'm going up into the woods and—*

The whistle of a steam engine ruptured the silence.

Keri tensed and closed her eyes.

As if beckoning her, the whistle screeched again.

Damn it. She marched around to the front of the lodge and stood at the top of the hill. The whistle howled twice more. *I heard you the first time.* Switching on the lantern, Keri Lange drew herself to her full height and charged into the mist.

The further she advanced, the warmer and more humid the air became until it was stifling. Her shirt clung to her skin. Clenching the wire handle of the lantern in her teeth, she slipped out of her jacket and tied it around her waist. Was the fog thinning up ahead? After a few more steps, she emerged into clear daylight and blistering heat. Beneath her feet, what was once the blacktop of Macartney Lane was nothing but grass and weeds. That was nowhere near as surprising as the railroad track that crossed her path no more than three yards ahead.

In the time it took Keri to process this, the passenger car from her vision was rolling into view around the curve to her right while the steam engine hauling at least three cars loaded with coal was blasting its whistle on a collision course from the left.

"Shit!" Keri whirled and plunged back into the fog. She darted up the hill, expecting the screech of brakes followed by the crack and thunder of the steam engine as it demolished the wooden passenger car. Keri imagined the screams and wails of the fifty people on board, the cries of the five children in Esther's care. She imagined these things, but heard none of them. The air cooled, the whistle faded. Halfway up the hill, Keri turned and raised her lantern but the fog was impenetrable.

By the time she trudged back up to the lodge, most of the writers had returned from their morning walks. A few were partaking of the continental breakfast set out by the staff in the kitchen adjacent to the lounge.

Carla glanced up as she scooped scrambled eggs onto her plate. "Good morning. We were worried you got lost in the fog."

"No, just took a short trip down the hill."

Barry sauntered over and poured himself a cup of coffee. "Did you run? You're drenched in sweat."

Keri started up the steps to her room. "Let's just say I was trying to catch a train."

"Close your eyes, plant your feet firmly on the ground with your palms on your thighs."

Seated on a couch between two other writers, it took every ounce of patience to stop herself from fidgeting as another guided meditation began. Keri closed her eyes and focused on the dulcet voice of the instructor. *Come on, get me back on that train.*

"Start by breathing in and out slowly three times..."

"I think Ms. Matthews is asleep."

Keri opened her eyes to find three-year-old Mary on her lap while Elizabeth and Sarah Rhody stared at her from the seat in front of hers.

"No, just resting my eyes. Where are we?"

"On the train," replied Bernadetta beside her.

Keri pulled Mary close and twisted in her seat. "Where's Billie?"

"Here." The girl popped up between the Rhody sisters.

A moment later, the tall man in grimy overalls made his way up the aisle, a wooden toolbox slung over his shoulder. He disappeared into a small room at the front of the car for a moment before returning empty-handed.

"We're comin' up to the curve," another passenger said. "Gettin' close to Wilpen."

The curve... Shit!

"Children, I need you to go into that little room."

Elizabeth followed her gaze. "The luggage compartment?"

"Why?" Billie asked.

"I'll explain later." Keri nudged Bernadetta into the aisle. A train whistle shrieked in the distance. "Just go now!"

Billie and the Rhody sisters bounded out of their seats and rushed up the center aisle.

"Esther, where are you takin' those kids?"

Keri ignored the question as Mary began to cry. She clutched the toddler close to her chest and hurried past several rows of seats.

"Was that whistle from our engine?" someone asked.

"Naw. Too far away," another replied. "Must be another train behind us."

In the doorway of the luggage compartment, Keri whirled. "Not behind us. In front of us! There's a freight train—"

The squeal of brakes swept her warning away.

A second later, the world exploded.

Keri flexed her hand in the grass, felt the soft blades between her fingers. She opened her eyes and winced against the sunlight. Somewhere nearby, a woman wailed. Overlapping voices shouted names. Chunks of coal and broken wood surrounded her. Several feet away, two bodies lay twisted and mangled. The closest one was familiar, although his face was turned away. Light blue shirt. White waistcoat and pleated pants. Once pristine, now stained black and crimson. The middle-aged man from the train platform.

Keri cocked her head and gaped at the steam engine that had toppled onto its side across the track. She slid her left forearm onto her stomach. Blood seeped from a series of gashes. An attempt to lift her right arm resulted in a flare of pain from shoulder to elbow.

"Mary..." She could muster little more than a hoarse whisper. After several deep breaths, she cried out again for the girl. When there was no response, she called each child's name.

"Ms. Matthews!"

Three bruised and battered faces appeared above her.

Keri cried out as she reached up with her left hand and brushed Billie's chin. "Thank God."

Bernadetta knelt beside her with a stunned Mary tucked in her arms. Both girls were covered in soot.

"Sarah," Keri whispered. "Elizabeth."

Bernadetta shook her head as tears streaked her face. Mary squirmed out of her arms and huddled against Keri.

"No..." Keri sobbed. "I'm sorry. I'm so sorry. I tried to save all of you."

"But you saved *us*." Billie lay down beside her. "Thank you."

"Breathe in... and breathe out. Breathe in... and breathe out."

Keri didn't wait for the meditation to end before slipping out of her seat and bolting up the steps to her room. With a few taps on her phone, she looked up the Wilpen train crash on two different websites. Whereas before there had been twenty-seven dead and twenty-six injured, those stats were now twenty-three and thirty, respectively. Of the children, only the Rhody sisters had perished. Esther Matthews was hailed a hero by the surviving passengers and the railroad's general manager.

That was of little comfort to Keri. She sat at the edge of the bed, lowered her head into her hands, and wept.

Foregoing a morning walk on the final day of the retreat, Keri showered, dressed, and plodded downstairs for breakfast. Most of the writers were either eating in the lounge while working on their projects or still out and about. She plucked a corn muffin from the basket and set it on her plate. While the rest of the food looked appealing, the previous day's experience had left her with little appetite. She poured a cup of coffee for herself and decided to sit alone on the front porch and take in the brisk autumn air. As she picked at her muffin, the front door of the lodge squeaked open.

"Good morning." Coffee in hand, Carla stopped at the table. "May I join you?"

"Of course."

"So did you find a new story to write?"

Keri returned a wan smile. "You could say the story found me."

"I'm not surprised. Every writer who comes here experiences a creative boost. I know I always do. Think you'll be back next year?"

"Absolutely. Like Barry said, there's a certain magic about this place. In just a few days, I've become attached to it." Keri fixed her gaze on the field at the bottom of the hill. "But before I leave, I think I'll pick some wildflowers down by the creek."

THE PERFECT ENDING

Gloria Bostic

Sage stared into space as she ran her fingers up and down the gnawed yellow pencil. It was better than staring at the blank page whose white face mocked her with emptiness. She tapped the pencil point on the paper then closed the journal around it and tossed them both on the wicker table by her side. Having traveled thousands of miles to escape all the real-life distractions that kept her from completing her second novel, she'd expected the words to finally flow like the Zambezi River rushed down Victoria Falls.

A pale moon sat alone in the Limpopo's winter sky, while the sun burned brightly. Sage sighed her surrender to its growing warmth. The writing could wait.

How can I write a silly mystery when I want only to absorb the wonders of this land?

She opened her eyes, breathed in the freshness, and listened to the silence interrupted only by the distant sounds of birds' banter. She knew beyond her sight were magnificent beasts unlike anything back home in Pennsylvania. Sage was beguiled by everything she saw... the colors of wheat and olives and honey and cinnamon...

Her quiet reverie was interrupted by the gray dance of monkeys just on the other side of the watering hole.

Amused by their antics, moments passed before she realized there was another presence. When had the zebra joined them? She strained to see more but dared not move for fear of startling the beautiful creature. Then she noticed movement. The mare nuzzled a still wobbly-legged newborn foal. Sage watched in wonder as the moments passed, knowing she was witness to one of Africa's many gifts.

The energy of the smile now lighting her face moved down her arm, and she reached for her journal.

She had been right to choose South Africa for her writing retreat after all. It wasn't until she had filled three pages that Sage paused. It was time to reach for her laptop.

"Miss Sage, dinner will be ready in about forty-five minutes." Asha, the cook at the lodge for many years, was one of the many sweet, considerate people who made her feel at home. "I'll put out some cheeses and biltong if you'd like... and a nice glass of wine before dinner?"

"Thank you, Asha. Cheese would be lovely, but no biltong for me, thanks." Sage had never acquired a taste for the cured meat that was so popular in the Limpopo Province. "And a glass of white, please?"

"Yes, would you like to have that out here? It's such a nice day."

"No, actually I've reached a good stopping point, and the sun is setting, so I think I'll put these things in my room and just come sit in the lodge with you, if that's okay." The sudden change in temperature with the setting of the sun still astonished her.

"Oh, my goodness, you know I always enjoy chatting with you." Asha giggled and added, "And I know you'll be needing to grab something warmer to put on now."

Sage jotted down a quick note before taking the few steps to her door, stowing her writing materials, and pulling on her cozy sweatshirt. When she looked in the mirror to comb her messed up long blonde hair, she couldn't help but grin. In big letters on the front of the hoody, it read, THIS IS WHAT A PUBLISHED AUTHOR LOOKS LIKE.

It was hard for Sage to believe, even now, that she could finally wear it proudly. A close friend had gifted her the sweatshirt a few months earlier when she published her first novel—a murder mystery. She had to pinch herself to make sure it was real, and it had been so well received. But could she do it again? Why was it so difficult to write the next one? This was supposed to be a series, after all.

But here she could get away from her roommate—who was sweet but lacked understanding of boundaries—endless dates with the wrong men, and looking for a marriage that would probably never happen. Here Sage could just focus on her other passion. Writing.

It was after dinner with her hosts, while they lingered over final sips of wine and comfortable conversation, when the van pulled in. A new group of weary visitors, just transported from the airport, tumbled out of the vehicle—three middle-aged men and a couple of much younger guys—all dragging their luggage and themselves to their rooms.

Within moments, four of the five men made their boisterous entrance into the main lodge and dining area before Sage had left the table. Only one of the younger men must have had the sense to call it a night.

Their hosts, Peter and Marli, welcomed the newcomers and, although it was obvious the men had been enjoying adult beverages all day long, offered them a nightcap.

"Where's Alexander?" Peter asked, setting four more glasses on the long table.

Amid a gaggle of laughter, the single young man in his mid-twenties said his buddy was already passed out on the bed in his room.

Not a good sign, was all Sage could think. These characters could totally ruin her quiet retreat. But then they would probably be gone most of the next day.

Sage stayed long enough not to appear rude, then made a quick retreat to her room. Though she loved the ambience of the ostrich egg lights on the wall, she flipped on the desk lamp to reread what she'd written that afternoon.

Yes, now we're getting somewhere.

With just two days left before she'd head back to the States, she hoped to keep up her momentum and finish the first draft by her self-imposed deadline.

The following morning, Sage strolled over to the lodge for her usual yogurt, hard-boiled egg, and a nice thick slice of peanut butter toast, before heading out for her morning walk around the compound. She noticed both trucks Peter typically took his clients out on were still parked in front of the lodge. *Odd*. She checked the time. It was after 7:00.

They must not be hunters. Hunting parties typically headed out early. Could this group all be there for photography? Birding?

When she returned about twenty-five minutes later and stopped in to say good morning to the workers who were busy making the lodge spotless, as they did every day, she found the man who'd been missing the night before sitting at the round breakfast table sipping from a large mug of coffee.

"Good morning, I'm Sage." She extended her hand, and the dark-haired man jumped to his full height of at least six feet.

"Nice to meet you. I'm Alex."

That was all the conversation Sage had planned on— even that being out of her introverted comfort zone—but Alexander invited her to join him for the meal. When she explained that she'd already eaten, he pleaded for her to at least have another cup of coffee.

She'd intended to have her second mug back in her room and focus on her manuscript until the sun moved around to her favorite spot, but again she didn't want to be rude. She would sit for a short visit, then bring her laptop and savor the warmth, the sights, and the sounds of the African birds and animals in the distance.

But sitting quietly with this extraordinarily good-looking, blue-eyed stranger—scary though it may be—had a certain appeal. Alexander looked to be about her age, and she hadn't seen a wedding ring, not that she was looking or anything...

Then she remembered what the other young man had said the night before. *He's already passed out on the bed in his room.* No, Sage had been down that road before, and the last thing she needed was another drunk in her life.

After a few sips from her mug and brief conversation about the beauty of South Africa, she excused herself and stood to leave.

"It was nice meeting you, Sage. See you later then."

Yes, she would see him of course at dinner, and perhaps even at lunch. Back outside she saw Peter striding down from the office area and the other group of gentlemen dragging toward the main lodge. A friendly wave to Peter, and she quickly ducked into her room. No need to get caught up in unnecessary conversation with the newcomers. This was her retreat, after all. Her escape from real-life distractions.

An hour later—after taking a little extra time with her hair and makeup—Sage relocated to her favorite writing spot. She was amazed at how much more intense the sun was in Africa, even in late June, their winter season.

After soaking up the rays for just a short time, she moved to the shady spot outside of her room and put total concentration on the end of the story that had begun unfolding itself overnight.

Having reached the point of greatest conflict, Sage was unaware of anything but the words that were flowing onto the page. She was unaware of Alex standing just feet away until he cleared his throat.

Her head jerked up, and with a gasp she said, "Oh, you scared me!" She had heard the vehicles leaving a while before and assumed she was now alone except for the staff.

"I'm so sorry. It's kind of hard not to sneak up on somebody here. I guess I'd better whistle as I approach next time."

"I suppose that would be a good idea," Sage said. *Next time? Does he think he's going to make a habit of this... whatever this is?* "I thought I heard you all leave. Aren't you going out today?" It was rare that a group of hunters arrived and didn't go out on their first full day.

"No, I'm not going anywhere."

"Oh, not hunting until tomorrow?"

"Not hunting at all." Alex grinned. "Not everyone who comes to South Africa is a hunter, you know."

"Well, of course I know that. I'm certainly not a hunter."

"So that makes two of us."

"Oh." Sage was momentarily at a loss for words. "So, what are you doing here?"

"What are you doing here?" Still wearing that flirtatious smile, Alex seemed to be baiting her.

Annoyed that he'd answered her question with a question, she replied, "Well, I'm an author, and I was writing before I was interrupted. I came here on a personal retreat... to escape annoying interruptions that keep me from completing my novel."

Alex took a step back. "And now I've become one of those annoyances. Pardon me. I'll let you get back to it." Still grinning, he turned sharply and headed around the corner of the building. He probably didn't even hear Sage's weak attempt at an apology.

Whatever. Within seconds, Sage was back into the thick of things with the characters on the page before her. It wasn't until she had reached the climax of the story that she finally paused and noticed it was close to the time Asha would be getting lunch on the table.

She stretched and meandered over to the main lodge.

"You're just in time," Asha said. "Mr. Alexander is washing up for lunch, and Marli said she'll be down in a few minutes. It will just be the four of us."

Sage loved when it was only Peter's wife and Asha there for lunch and Asha could sit down and enjoy the meal with them, but Alex? Why?

By the time she had washed up and returned to the dining room, everyone was ready to sit down to the meal, including the annoying newcomer. She was greeted warmly by the other two women and got a rather cool good afternoon from the gentleman.

After the blessing, Marli asked a simple question.

"So how is the story coming along?"

"It's coming," Alex said before Sage could answer.

Her head snapped up, and she threw him a look that she hoped conveyed annoyance. How dare he answer for her! And how would he know how her story was evolving? *And what's with the smirk?*

"Good," Marli said. "And how about you, Sage? How are you doing with your novel?"

Wait... what?

"Oh, it... it's good. I'm quite happy with the way it's flowing these last couple of days."

"Wonderful." Marli took a sip of juice. "This is the first time we've ever had two writers here at the same time."

Two writers? Oh no!

"So, you're a writer too, Alex?" Sage gave him a sheepish smile when he nodded, and her own smile was answered with a hardy laugh.

"You didn't know?" Asha asked. "Oh yes, Mr. Alex has written many books. Tell her about the one you're writing now."

"Oh, I don't want to bore her with that." Alex took another bite of his lunch, but with a little more urging he was persuaded to share that he was working on an historical fiction set in South Africa.

Sage made a mental note to look for his books online after lunch. "So, you're not a hunter after all."

"No. Neither is my buddy, Bob. He's a photojournalist working on an article about the poaching problem here.

The other three guys are the hunters. We just met on the flight over."

By the time they'd finished their last bite and were pushing their chairs back from the table, Alex seemed to have forgotten how rudely Sage had treated him earlier, but she was still kicking herself for the haughty way she'd stated that she was an author.

Once she returned to her room and checked Alexander Drakos's body of work, she felt even more ridiculous. His last six books, all bestsellers, dwarfed her accomplishments. Her sweatshirt might say she was a published author, but she felt like such a fraud.

It was her habit to take another short stroll after lunch to meditate and bring her mind and energy back to creating new words, so she put on her walking shoes, pulled her hair back in a ponytail, grabbed her hat, and set out to do just that. With not a cloud in the sky, Sage marveled at the depth of blue and the vastness of the land beyond. This world, so different from her own, was yet like a second home. As she listened to the lone African mourning dove, she felt the welcoming arms of Africa. It was a place like no other.

You've got to be kidding me.

As she went around the bend, there he was again. *Is this man everywhere?*

Alex had been concentrating on something off in the distance, and when he heard her, he put a hand up, palm toward her, and with his other hand, put a finger to his lips. Then he pointed in the direction he'd been looking.

Sage's gaze followed his until she saw them. There, not twenty yards away, stood the zebra with her day-old baby by her side. Barely breathing, she watched in awe until the ever-vigilant mother nudged her newborn farther into the brush.

"There's nothing like it, is there?" Alex wiped the sweat off his forehead with the back of his hand.

"It's quite magical." Standing there now, that magic was fading as she felt the perspiration between her breasts. Though she hadn't walked far, she'd had her limit of Africa's intense afternoon sun and turned back toward the lodge. She heard Alex's footfalls behind her and glanced over her shoulder.

"I'm not following you, I swear." He threw his hands up. "I've just got to find some shade before I melt."

Sage had to laugh at his reaction. And actually, that devilish smile was kind of cute. *Too bad he drinks.*

They walked in uncomfortable silence—though Sage sensed some kind of energy between them—until turning onto separate paths to their respective rooms. She glanced back at the same unfortunate moment that Alex chose to look up at her.

"See you later," he called over his shoulder, and she heard him chuckle.

Dinner wasn't until after 7:00 that evening as they waited for Peter and his clients to return, so Sage was sitting at the round table enjoying snacks and a glass of Amarula when Alex strolled in.

"How's the book coming?" he asked, taking the seat next to her. "Making progress?"

"As a matter of fact, this afternoon was quite productive. I'm ready to work on the denouement." Unsure whether he was truly interested or mocking her, she added, "And how about you? How is your book coming along?"

"I'm still at the outline stage and doing a lot of research for this one, but making progress. There's nothing better than visiting the actual place you're writing about to get the feel of it."

"So, have you visited all the countries where your books are set? Even Australia?"

"Oh, so you've read my books?"

"No, I just, um—"

"Ah, you were checking up on me." There was that laugh again, but she couldn't deny it.

"Well, yes. I was kind of curious."

"Thank you, Asha," he said when she brought him an orange Fanta.

"No wine this evening?" Sage asked, wondering if he hadn't quite gotten over the other night.

"No, I don't drink. Back to your question about Australia though, yes, and you'd love it."

Doesn't drink? Why would he lie about that?

Their conversation was interrupted by the arrival of the hunting party who had cleaned up and were ready to eat, drink, and be merry. As they gathered around the table, Peter filled each man's wine glass—skipping Alex without asking—then said the blessing.

The young photojournalist and Alex sat across from Sage, who was in her usual place by Marli. She couldn't hear a lot of their conversation but did notice what a hearty appetite both men had and that Alex had glanced her way more times than would be expected by someone just looking around the table.

Once, when their eyes met, their gaze held just long enough to be awkward. And then he smiled. *That smile...*

The following day as Sage was writing the final scene of her novel—a sweet, steamy love scene—her heroine, Felicity, fell into the arms of the hero, Detective Zachary

Moore. She looked into Zachary's eyes, traced the smile on his lips, and finally felt those lips on hers.

A chill ran down Sage's spine. It wasn't Zachary's lips she envisioned. It was Alex's.

No! Stop it! Having been down that road before, she vowed never again. Besides, hadn't he told a bold-faced lie? *"He's already passed out on the bed..."* they had said.

On one hand, she decided she would have to avoid Alex until leaving for home tomorrow. On the other, she wondered why she hadn't seen him that morning.

At lunch she got the answer to the latter question. Marli said he went to meet with an English gentleman in the nearby town of Modimolle and wouldn't be back until dinner. Knowing she should be relieved, Sage felt only disappointment.

"You know, I'm a little confused," she said to Marli and Asha over lunch. "I wonder why Alex told me he doesn't drink."

"He doesn't," the other two women replied in unison.

"But... but, that first night... when they arrived. They had all been drinking, and his friend said he passed out."

When Marli and Asha finished laughing, it was Marli who replied. "They meant he was passed out from exhaustion. Alex just got back from a trip to Costa Rica the day before. He was worn out from all the traveling."

Amid her feelings of embarrassment for misjudging him and relief that she had been wrong, came the memory of Felicity and Zachary—as she replaced them with herself and Alexander.

That night at dinner, when she caught Alex looking her way, she didn't avert her eyes. She held his gaze and returned his smile. She saw the question in his expression, and she vowed to answer it before leaving the next morning.

It was several hours later, after they had gathered around the fire pit when slowly, one by one, the others retired for the evening. Sage and Alex were finally alone together.

"Something has changed," Alex said.

"Yes, it has." Sage reached over and traced his lips with her finger... and then she waited for what she knew would come next. She wasn't disappointed.

CONTRIBUTORS

LORRAINE DONOHUE BONZELET is a graduate of Steven's Institute of Technology, The Institute of Children's Literature, Dr. Mira Reisberg's Children's Book Academy, and a long-time member of the Society of Children's Book Writers and Illustrators. Lorraine is a picture book enthusiast and mindful writer. She has a non-fiction article and photographs published in *Boys' Quest* magazine, "Unusual Sports." She's also published in the Mindful Writers Retreat Anthologies: *Into the Woods, Over the River and Through the Woods, Love on the Edge,* and *Shell House.* Lorraine and her husband (and their daughters who are always welcome to pop in) are newcomers to the Blue Ridge Mountains in Virginia where they enjoy lake-life, kayaking, hiking, birdwatching, and stargazing. Lorraine loves nothing more than spending precious time vacationing with her family while her two tabby cats throw wild hairball-hurling parties at the house. Lorraine recently rekindled her passion for art which has sparked many new story ideas. Stay tuned...

GLORIA BOSTIC lives in York County, Pennsylvania, with Lee, her husband of thirty-seven years. Her greatest joy is spending time with family, especially her three sons, four grandchildren, and sister. Bostic is an active member of the American Legion Auxiliary who prays for peace, supports our troops, and serves our veterans who have sacrificed so much for our freedom. Since retiring from her career as a special education teacher, supervisor, and psychologist, Bostic has published one children's picture book and eight inspirational romance novels and three Christmas novellas, all of which can be found on Amazon and in several local libraries. This is her third contribution to the Mindful Writers Retreat Series. gkbostic.com Facebook @gkbostic

DEBORAH HETRICK CATANESE, a lifelong Pittsburgher, business owner, and avid traveler, holds a BA in English and an MS in Information Science from the University of Pittsburgh. Her articles, poetry, and Creative Nonfiction pieces have been featured in the *Pittsburgh Post-Gazette*, Project Motherhood blog, Carlow University's *Voices in the Attic*, *Watershed Journal*, Beautiful Cadaver project, Ekphrastic Review, *But You Don't Look Sick* by IndieBlu(e), and numerous blog posts for Online Mindful Writers Group. She has received numerous poetry awards from *Konect* E-zine. Deborah's publications include three fundraising books: *The Green Turtle Cookbook*; *Gilda's Club Presents Zelda's Kitchen*; and *ACK Poetically*, a poetry collection by her late friend Del Wynn. She was thrilled to join Mindful Writers in the delightful *Shell House* with her nonfiction story "Slaughter Beach." Her story "Fair Winds and Following Seas" is Deborah's first published work of fiction.

JENNIFER D. DIAMOND is a speech therapist turned international award-winning author. When she's not reading, writing, or paddle-boarding, Diamond enjoys boating with her husband and rescue pup in the heart of Pennsylvania. jenniferddiamondwriter.wordpress.com

Facebook @Jennifer.D.Diamond.writer
Instagram @jennifer_d_diamond_writer

JUDY ENGLAND-McCARTHY is both an author and professional storyteller. Her creative intention is to entertain and transform people through her stories. Judy's professional career as a storyteller commenced in 2009 and as an author in 2013. One of her poems was presented in video format for "The Just Listening Project" and another poem won 1st place at Fanstory.com. Her book *Amazing Petunia's Adventures* is being made into an animation. Other books by this author are *Twas Midnight* and *Why Oh Why Did the Witch Swallow a Fly?* This is her 4th anthology and her 2nd with Mindful Writers Retreat Series. Beginwithastory.com

PHIL GIUNTA's novels include the paranormal mysteries *Testing the Prisoner*, *By Your Side*, and *Like Mother, Like Daughters*. His short stories appear in two dozen anthologies of science fiction, fantasy, horror, and more. He is a multiple award-winning author and member of the Horror Writers Association, the National Federation of Press Women, and the Greater Lehigh Valley Writers Group. Phil is currently working on his fourth paranormal mystery novel while plotting his triumphant escape from the pressures of corporate America where he has been imprisoned for thirty years. www.philgiunta.com.
Facebook @writerphilgiunta
Instagram @phil_giunta71
BlueSky @philgiunta.bsky.social

KIMBERLY KURTH GRAY was born and raised in Baltimore where she finds daily inspiration for her writing. The winner of the William F. Deeck-Malice

Domestic 2009 Grant for Unpublished Writers and a 2017 Hruska Fellowship, she is a member of Sisters in Crime, Guppies, and Pennwriters. She has recently published two novellas, *North by North Pole Beach* and *Dial M for Mother-in-Law*. Her short stories have been published in Cat and Mouse Press and Level Best Anthologies. In addition to working on a historical novel and writing short stories, she writes The Detective's Daughter on the blog Scenes from a Baltimore Kitchen at www.baltimorebound.me.

HILARY HAUCK is an Italian-speaking Brit living in the U.S. Dubbed "an extraordinary novel" by The Midwest Book Review, her debut novel, *From Ashes to Song*, was inspired by the true story of three Italians who immigrated to Pennsylvania ninety years before she did. As a young adult, Hilary moved to Italy from her native UK where she mastered the language, learned how to cook food she can no longer eat, and won a national karate championship. After meeting her husband, she moved to the U.S. in 2002, where she learned the craft of writing, the art of leadership, and at last lay her imposter syndrome to rest. Her stories and poems have appeared in anthologies in the Mindful Writers Retreat Series, *Like Sunshine After Rain*, *The Ekphrastic Review*, *Balloons Lit Journal*, and *Centered* magazine. Hilary lives on a small patch of woods in rural Pennsylvania with her husband and a cat with a penchant for laundry. Visit her at www.hilaryhauck.com.

CINDY HILL (MOLDOVAN) was born and raised in the tropical paradise of Belize, Central America, until the age of seventeen, when she moved to Houston, Texas. In her memoir, *Growing Up Third World*, Cindy wrote about her experience moving from Belize to the United States and often shares funny and real stories of what it was like growing up in a large family with ten siblings. She attended Lee College of nursing in Baytown, Texas, and worked in Houston for twenty-five years until she retired from the medical field of nursing. She followed her passion for writing and is now a published author. The proud mother of three adult daughters and grandmother of four, she is passionate about her family, often visiting them in Texas and South Carolina for long conversations, priceless hugs and kisses, and sweet stories from any of her four grandchildren.

DONNA LUCAS is a poet, humorist, essayist, and short fiction author. She blogs at Days of Part-Time Sunshine and has been a guest host for Mindful Writers Group. She is a lifelong learner who holds a BS in English Education, an MA in English, and an MFA in Creative Writing. She has taught English Language Arts for 30 years and is currently a middle school writing teacher and creative writing club coach. Donna lives in Meadville, Pennsylvania, with her husband, two daughters, two dogs, and one kitty. She is a people person who loves talking to others, listening to their stories, and telling her own. parttimesunshine.com

Author **CAROLYN MENKE** moved around the country growing up but every summer she and her family make their way back to the beach. A graduate of Carnegie Mellon University, Carolyn is the author of *Return to Me*, a WWII historical novel, and *I'm Yours*, a Roaring Twenties novella. Her nonfiction has been featured in *Pittsburgh Magazine*. Carolyn teaches English language arts and creative writing to children around the world, in addition to college admissions consulting. She looks forward to her next trip to the coast with her husband, three daughters, and goldendoodle to visit Grandma and Grandpa along with aunts, uncles, and cousins who will undoubtedly jockey for bunk beds and surfboards.

AMY MORLEY is a fiction author and poet whose stories have been published in all previous volumes of the Mindful Writers Retreat Series anthologies. Her poetry chapbook "The Hour Has Come" was featured in *The Ninth Room*, a narrative in verse told through the collective minds of ten international authors which debuted at #1 New Release in June 2021. When she's not writing, you can find her in her hot pink Fiat convertible coasting through the Delmarva Peninsula with her Yorkshire Terrier, Daphney. Follow her travel writing adventures on Facebook. @AmyMorleyAuthor

CAROL SCHOENIG lives in Cranberry Township, Pennsylvania, with her husband of fifty-four years and a golden doodle named Millie.

Bestselling author, KATHLEEN SHOOP, holds a PhD in reading education and has more than twenty years of experience in the classroom. She writes historical fiction, women's fiction, and romance. Shoop's novels have garnered various awards in the Independent Publisher Book Awards (IPPY), Eric Hoffer Book Awards, Indie Excellence Awards, Next Generation Indie Book Awards, Readers' Favorite, and the San Francisco Book Festival. Kathleen has been featured in *USA Today* and the *Writer's Guide to 2013*. Her work has appeared in *The Tribune-Review*, four *Chicken Soup for the Soul* books, and *Pittsburgh Parent* magazine. Kathleen coordinates

Mindful Writing Retreats and is a regular presenter at conferences for writers. She lives in Oakmont, Pennsylvania, with her husband and two children. www.kshoop.com Facebook @Kathleen Shoop

MELINDA TAULER lives in the mountains of West Virginia with her husband, children, and menagerie of animals. She is in the process of publishing her first novel, *The Accidental Hitman*, a story which features the communication between people and crows. She discovered her passion for telling stories after winning a school writing contest in the third grade.

LISA VALLI, a certified financial planner and benefits consultant, has been featured in *INC Magazine* and Who's Who of American Women for her professional achievements. But she also enjoys exercising her "right brain" by creating stories. She is a member of various writers' organizations and is currently working on a story inspired by her trips to nearby Deep Creek Lake, Maryland. She resides in Venetia, Pennsylvania, with her husband, two daughters and their little dog, Crosby (named after Sidney, of course).

DENISE WEAVER, a *summa cum laude* graduate of the University of Pittsburgh, is a former library director. A love of sharing food and stories, along with a penchant for photography and research, make a winning combination that inspires her to write. She has more than 250 nonfiction articles published in local and regional magazines and is delving into the world of short stories. She once conquered her fear of public performances and sang on-stage at Carnegie Hall. Denise and her husband split their time between the beautiful Laurel Highlands of

Pennsylvania and the irresistible pull of the Sunshine State. www.deniseweaver.com

MICHELE SAVAUNAH ZIRKLE, MA, PhD, is a published author, high school teacher and holistic energy practitioner who enjoys sharing innovative ways to break through writing barriers and to live a creative life. She is the author of *Rain No Evil*. In addition to hosting "Life Speaks," on Appalachian Independent Radio, Michele leads meditations and healing events, inspiring participants to live with passion and purpose. Her short stories have appeared in *Mountain Ink Literary Journal* and vignettes in *The Journal of Health and Human Experience*. She presents writing workshops for West Virginia Writer's Inc. and Northern Appalachia Writer's Conferences. She is a graduate of Concord University, Marshall Graduate School, and The Institute of Metaphysical Humanistic Science. www.michelezirkle.com Facebook @ZirksQuirks

Also by

MINDFUL WRITERS RETREAT AUTHORS

Into the Woods (Book 1)
Short stories, poems, essays, music, and one walking meditation. Each piece is unique in tone and genre and the result is that the collection captures the fascinating, frightening, fun, healing, and fantastical wonder of time spent in the woods. The twenty-six contributors who attend Mindful Writers Retreats in the mountains of Ligonier, Pennsylvania, are donating one hundred percent of the proceeds to support the research and work of The Children's Heart Foundation.

Over the River and Through the Woods (Book 2)
A holiday pastiche from the authors of Mindful Writers Retreat, sure to light your festive candles! From a Thanksgiving snowstorm that mends old feuds... to the family misunderstandings that fuel new ones... a quirky elf and some romantic stardust will get you ready to go *Over the River and Through the Woods* on a journey through time!

Love on the Edge (Book 3)

From love in the time of war to love at first sight and long walks in the snow... to sparks flying because of nosy neighbors... *Love on the Edge* reveals the essence and evolution of human relationships, written in a time when we're all searching for deeper meaning and connection.

Shell House (Book 4)

A compelling new beach read. Beautifully situated between the Atlantic Ocean and Silver Lake, this magnificent home is the perfect setting for inner transformation and life-changing beach memories. From the Roaring '20s to modern times, the shifting sands lend a glorious backdrop to intrigue, bootlegging, a séance, an alien visit, and true love as precious as hidden treasure.

Wedding Season (Book 5)

An intoxicating blend of the condition of love with the excitement of Rehoboth Beach and all manner of nuptial ceremonies. Short and sweet tales feature meet-cutes with dogs on the beach, rock star love, reignited passions, mistaken identity, blessings from long-gone relatives, insta-love, longtime-coming love, warm families, raucous members of the wedding party, and more!